P9-DXS-797

WITHDRAWN

LONDON
PUBLIC LIBRARY
AND
ART MUSEUM

THE RULE OF THIRDS

THE
RULE
OF
THIRDS

Chantel Guertin

ECW Press

LONDON PUBLIC LIBRARY

Copyright © Chantel Guertin, 2013

All rights reserved. No part of this publication may be reproduced, stored in a retrieval system, or transmitted in any form by any process — electronic, mechanical, photocopying, recording, or otherwise — without the prior written permission of the copyright owners and ECW Press. The scanning, uploading, and distribution of this book via the Internet or via any other means without the permission of the publisher is illegal and punishable by law. Please purchase only authorized electronic editions, and do not participate in or encourage electronic piracy of copyrighted materials. Your support of the author's rights is appreciated.

This is a work of fiction. Names, characters, places, and incidents either are the product of the author's imagination or are used fictitiously, and any resemblance to actual persons, living or dead, business establishments, events, or locales is entirely coincidental.

Published by ECW Press
2120 Queen Street East, Suite 200,
Toronto, Ontario, Canada M4E 1E2
416-694-3348 / info@ecwpress.com

Library and Archives Canada
Cataloguing in Publication

Guertin, Chantel, 1976–, author
The rule of thirds / Chantel Guertin.

ISBN 978-1-77041-159-3 (pbk.)
Also issued as: 978-1-77090-462-0
(PDF); 978-1-77090-463-7 (ePub)

I. Title.

PS8613.U4684R84 2013
jC813'.6   C2013-902469-7

Editor for the press: Crissy Calhoun
Cover design: Carolyn McNeillie
Cover images: Tallent Tam,
www.tallentsblog.com
Author photo: Steven Khan
Printing: Friesens 5 4 3 2 1

The publication of *The Rule of Thirds* has been generously supported by the Canada Council for the Arts which last year invested $157 million to bring the arts to Canadians throughout the country, and by the Ontario Arts Council (OAC), an agency of the Government of Ontario, which last year funded 1,681 individual artists and 1,125 organizations in 216 communities across Ontario for a total of $52.8 million. We also acknowledge the financial support of the Government of Canada through the Canada Book Fund for our publishing activities, and the contribution of the Government of Ontario through the Ontario Book Publishing Tax Credit and the Ontario Media Development Corporation.

PRINTED AND BOUND IN CANADA

For CMS
Love MCG

And in memory of my mom

"Can you Photoshop this?" Dace asks. She strides into the school's photocopy room and tosses a paper at me. "Algebra test."

I finish adjusting the aperture on my camera and then glance at the paper. "You got a D."

"Thanks for the newsflash. Pippa Greene, ace reporter. You really earn your keep here on the school paper," she says, hopping up onto the table in front of me and crossing her legs under her, yoga-style.

Photocopiers line the walls around the room leaving a rectangle of space in the room's middle where a couple of tables are pushed together. In our budget-stretched school, the photocopier room happens to be the headquarters of the school newspaper, where I'm the photo editor, and of the photo club, where I'm president. The flatscreens of five iMacs form a line on one side of the tables. The other side is just open space, where we can lay out the proofs of the paper, or plug in our laptops.

(Not that I have one.)

(Although I'm planning on rectifying that with the prize money from a certain photography competition.)

(More on that later.)

"Are you in photo club? Are you on the *Hall Pass* masthead?" Jeffrey Manson grumbles from behind the computer directly behind Dace. "Oh no? You're not? Then why are you in here?"

"How'd you get a D?" I ask Dace, then snap a pic of her as she sweeps her long blonde hair up into a topknot, then secures it with an elastic that's hidden under a stash of colorful rubber bracelets on her wrist. She's wearing her usual: leggings (black today), loose T-shirt (gray) and black motorcycle boots.

She shrugs. "Dunno. I'm not into algebra. And I'm busy with go-sees. Vivs can't find out about this," Dace says. "If I get below a B on anything, I have to skip a go-see or turn down a job. Which is so ridiculous, don't even get me started, because hello, what's going to get me further in life, modeling or knowing how to dissect a frog?"

She has *really* not been paying attention in algebra.

"What exactly do you want me to do with this?"

"Change the D to an A?" she says hopefully.

I give her a look.

"Like, scan it and do it in Photoshop?" Dace suggests.

"No problem, but your mom will be able to tell it's a printout, not a pen mark. She's ace at that stuff."

"So I email her the file and tell her the school's saving paper."

"Are you serious? Just do what you usually do." Which is fake her mom's signature. "Or—here's a crazy idea, Dace, why don't you tell her the truth? She's going to find out eventually."

I hand the test back to her as the paper's assistant editor walks into the room. "Plus, I don't have time—I've got an editorial meeting for *Hall Pass* in 10 minutes, then my volunteer assessment with the Glumster at 4."

"Oh god, don't even remind me. I have my first shift in half an hour. Helping bratty little kids? And on a Friday afternoon? Kill me now."

Everyone at Spalding High has to complete 120 volunteer hours to graduate, starting in our junior year. Dace's placement is at the after-school homework club at the library. It doesn't sound all that bad to me. There are worse placements. Much worse.

"I bet you'll be great, Dace. You're really fun, and funny—the kids will love you."

"I just hope you get placed with me," Dace says. I sigh. I'm sort of dreading having to add another thing to my life. It's not that I don't want to help other people, but things are going to be insane until after Vantage Point. The photography competition I mentioned. *The* photography competition—less than three weeks away, and whether I win or lose will alter the course of my life.

No biggie or anything.

Dace's iPhone buzzes and she looks down at the text. "Shut the front door." Dace is going 30 days without swearing. Or trying to—it's only day 3.

I try to peer over the top of her phone to see. "What's up?"

"Elise wants to book me for a car show in *Cheektowaga*. This is insane. I don't do car shows. Thank god for that D—my mom's wrath could save me . . ."

"Why is Elise even booking you for a car show?" The whole reason Dace changed agents was so she could get higher profile, more glam gigs. No more mall shows, no more department store catalogs.

"Don't do the car show," a voice says from the door. I look past Dace as she swivels around. The guy in the door looks like he should be standing in the entrance to Abercrombie—minus that cologne that totally reeks when you walk past the store. His sandy blond hair is cut so that it's purposely messy, and his blue eyes are piercing. Swoon.

"Who asked you?" Dace says. She pulls her hair out of the topknot.

"I'm no expert," Abercrombie says, "but you look like you're way too good for Cheektowaga."

Dace looks him up and down. "I like you already. But who *are* you?"

"Another person who's not supposed to be in here," Jeffrey grumbles.

"Ben Baxter," says the newcomer. Even better.

I've always wished I had a double-consonant name. Like Pippa Price. Pippa Prince. Actually, nevermind. Those sound like stripper names. "Just moved here from Buffalo—very close to Cheektowaga. And I can confidently tell you you're too good for that town." He turns to me. "And you must be Pippa Greene."

"Uh . . ." The heat in my cheeks is enough to make me sweat. Huh—it's not bad enough that he sees me blush, I have to start *sweating* too?

"Mrs. Edmonson said you're in charge of the photography club? Nice digs." He looks around at the photocopiers, takes off his cross-body bag and lays it on the table. It sits there amid the paper reams and the toner cartridges. The pebbling in the leather looks expensive. Who has a leather bag in high school?

"Budget cuts," I explain. "The usual. And hey, if photography doesn't work out for us, at least we'll know how to photocopy."

"We all have bright careers ahead of us," Jeffrey finishes. "As secretaries."

Ben ignores us. "Well, anyway, I know it's three weeks into the term—but I just heard about the big photography competition and apparently I've got to actually be in photo club to enter? Mrs. Edmonson says you're pretty hard-ass about who gets in, that there are only five members? So . . . what are my chances of coercing you to take a very talented senior as your sixth?" He winks at me.

Dace mouths *Oh my god* and makes a face. I can feel her willing me to let him in.

"You can join if you want," I say.

"Sweet. So tell me about this competition. What've I got to do to win the five grand?"

"You're not going to," Dace says. "Pippa's going to win, and when she's at the superstar Tisch camp in NYC I'm going to go with her for moral support." She grins. What Dace really means is she'll crash in my dorm room so she can go shopping. Not that it won't be fun to have her there. "You should see her stuff," Dace continues. "She's going to be a fashion photographer and we'll travel the world together. She'll shoot all my *Vogue* covers."

"Fashion, huh?" Ben says to me, and I nod without hesitation because I know Dace is watching. It's been our plan for years—Dace the model, me the photographer, tag-team tandem. Except I have a new theme for my competition portfolio, one I've been working on for months. Dace doesn't know. I guess she'll find out soon enough.

"Mrs. Edmonson said you were good," Ben says.

"Good?" Dace says. "Pippa won the freshman/sophomore division last year. She *started* the photo club. And she's the best photographer in it."

"Thanks a lot," Jeffrey pipes up from beside me. I thought he'd totally tuned us out.

"She's biased," I say. And Jeffrey Manson's my stiffest competition at Spalding for sure. Even though he only got an honorable mention last year, he was in the junior/senior division—and the only students who beat him were seniors. So there's a really good chance he'll place this year. He's going with the same theme as last year: "Found." His photos are technically flawless, but I can't help being skeptical about just how many lonely shoes or gloves or socks there are lying around this (pretty small) town. I think he might be helping his cause.

"Why don't I judge for myself?" Ben picks up my camera, turning it over in his well-manicured hands. Seriously, not a cuticle out of place, and here I am biting my nails. I tuck my hands under my legs and look at Dace. She mouths the word *hot* and I try not to laugh.

He snaps a picture of me, then holds the camera back to see. "Gorgeous," he says, and I'm not sure if he's talking about the photo or me, but Dace calls him on it.

"Smooth one, Ben Baxter," she says as she jumps off the table, then shoves her algebra test into her bag. "Wish me luck in jail. I mean, the *library*."

Meanwhile Ben's snapped another picture of me. He hands my camera back, and I look at the pic. At least my long brown hair—which is usually annoyingly wavy—is still straight from my flat-iron session this morning. "You're really photogenic," he says, and I feel myself blushing (again). "And you've got good taste. I've got the same camera."

"Really?" I say, then cringe at how ridiculous I sound. It's a Canon Rebel. It's like the Heinz of ketchup. Everyone has this camera. It's not like it's my retro Nikon—the one Dad gave me. Which is actually in my bag, but I don't mention it. I don't like letting anyone get their hands on it.

Lisa Rui, who's the paper's editor-in-chief, rushes into the room. She's wearing her uniform: white button-down shirt, buttoned-up cardigan, her shiny black hair pulled back in a take-me-seriously low ponytail and a pencil tucked behind her ear. She's been wearing variations on the same outfit ever since she became editor-in-chief.

"All right, let's get started," she says, out of breath, her brow furrowed. She's always stressed out, as though she's running the *New York Times*, not the student paper. Three sophomore girls rush in behind her and grab seats around the table.

"*Hall Pass* meeting," I explain to Ben.

"No problem. So . . . when does photo club meet?"

"Tuesdays at lunch. We pick a theme every week and show our photos the next. This week is gray. If you want to show anything."

He looks concerned.

"Totally no pressure, though. And you can just show pics you've already taken. Doesn't have to be new stuff."

He puts a hand on my shoulder and my pulse quickens. "OK—sounds good. See you then." He swings his bag over his shoulder and then he's gone.

Lisa starts the meeting by telling us this year we *have* to make sure everyone makes it into the paper at least once. That Mrs. Edmonson is adamant.

"Just put them in the Streeters," Ed, the deputy editor, says. The Streeters column is my thing— every two weeks I feature four students on the back page of the paper. I take a pic and ask them some timely question. Like who they think is going to win the football game on Friday, or what they ate for lunch in the caf. You know, *hard news*.

"Pippa, are we clear?" Lisa asks.

"Yep. No problem."

Perfect excuse to take Ben Baxter's picture.

●　●　●

My cellphone blasts "Who Let the Dogs Out?" as I'm walking out Spalding High School's front doors. The bright afternoon sun basically spotlights my embarrassment. Has anyone heard? I scrabble around in my bag to find my phone and silence it as quickly as possible. My mom got a job as a vet assistant at Furry Friendz and comes home smelling like dog breath. Hence the special ringtone—but the joke's on me because my mom doesn't ever hear it ring. Because she's calling me. And I end up looking like The Girl Who's into Super-Lame Songs, Circa 2000. I find my phone just at the part where the singer goes, "Who? Who? Who?" Or is it: "Woof! Woof! Woof!" I've heard the refrain about a billion times and I still can't tell. There's a brief moment where I consider not answering it. I do not want to have The Conversation About the Worst Volunteer Assessment Meeting in the History of Volunteer Assessment Meetings. But Mom pays for my phone, and she has a rule about it.

MOM'S PHONE RULES
1. Answer when she calls.

"How did it go?" Mom asks, a little too eagerly.
"Not good."
"Not well," she corrects me.

"Same diff." *Ack! Of course it isn't the same!* Did I say "not good" in my assessment? Is that the reason I got the absolute worst placement ever?

"I'll pick you up and you can tell me all about it."

"Don't bother," I say miserably, holding the phone away from my face to check the time: 4:45. "The stupid volunteer orientation is in 15 minutes." As soon as the words are out of my mouth, I regret them. For one thing, if I hadn't told her, there'd still be a chance I could ditch the orientation and buy myself some time to convince the Glumster to give me a different placement. Because I do not want to tell Mom where my placement is. And she's going to ask. And Mom has a rule about lying.

MOM'S RULES ABOUT LYING
1. Don't.

"Oh, I'll drive you. I'm passing right by," she says, quite literally I realize, when a moment later, a horn honks and I see my mother's beat-up brown Honda Accord pull up beside me on Elm. I can't say I'm disappointed—my red wedges are killing me. No one ever said wearing cute shoes was a cakewalk.

I lean through the open window, being careful not to get my white blazer dirty. Mom's wearing her green scrubs, which means she's either on her way to—or home from—the clinic. "Can I drive?" I ask hopefully.

"Not a chance," Mom says, her pale skin crinkling at the corner of her eyes as she smiles.

"Big surprise." I open the passenger-side door

and get in. I have my learner's permit and my mom used to be great about practicing with me, but ever since—well, anyway, in the last couple of months she's pulled back on letting me get behind the wheel. Says it's too dangerous. Seriously, the DMV should make some sort of rule that parents *have* to let their kids drive once they get their learner's.

"So where's your placement?" Mom asks as she pulls away from the curb.

I exhale, then inhale, then spit it out. "St. Christopher's."

My smile—I think it seems fine. I have to be fine so that she'll be fine. But she's not fine. She doesn't say anything for a moment and then pulls over to the side of the road and puts the car in park. She hits the hazard lights button and stares straight ahead. The lights click loudly as they flick on and off. Why do they do that anyway? Can't they make hazard lights quieter? I consider turning on the radio, to fill in the silence. She's biting her lip in the way that she does. Her red hair looks nice today. She curled it. That's a good sign. I don't think she's curled it in months. The clock on the dashboard changes to 4:51. She takes a deep breath, then lets it out and turns to face me.

"Oh Pippa."

"It's fine!" I say, overselling it. "It's actually really good. It's fine."

"Are you sure?" She's really studying me.

"It's fine. Listen, at least I know the place, right?" The clock turns to 4:52.

"Mom, I need to get there."

Her look lingers on me but I stay firm. I'm fine.

I'm fine. I'm fine. And just as I'm about to not be fine my mom turns back in her seat and shifts the Honda into gear.

She almost misses Greenwood Avenue.

"Mom, the turn!" I say, and we squeal through a left turn, narrowly missing a truck from Pete's Towing.

"Why don't I park and go in with you? Might make it easier."

"And become the girl whose mom came with her to the orientation meeting?" I shake my head. "No. I'm *fine*."

"Oh honey. OK. I said I'd cover one of the other girls who called in sick tonight, but I'll pop a pizza in the oven for dinner. You'll just have to warm it up when you get home."

Friday night has been pizza night forever, but in the past three months, Mom switched from real pizza to frozen. It's like eating the box, instead of the pizza. But now is not the right moment to make fun of her about it.

"OK," I say, and lean over for a hug.

"Listen, if you're not OK with this then I can have a talk with the Bumster. We can get you another volunteer assignment. It'd be no problem."

"The *Glumster*, Mom. Mr. Gloucester's nickname is the Glumster. I'll be fine. Come say goodnight when you get home. I'll be up working on my Vantage Point entry."

My bag bounces all over the place as I take the steps to the hospital two at a time. I know she's watching me, so halfway up the steps I turn and wave like "Hey! No big deal! Don't worry about me!"

She waves back and drives away. The sliding doors open with a whoosh and a wave of cold air hits me.

It's been three months since I've been here.

Am I OK with this?

"You can't stand there," barks a security guard. The doors slide closed again behind me, then open, then closed, but I'm frozen. My head spins. Everything's starting to go black. I manage to back up, one step behind the other until I'm outside again. I sit on the top concrete step; my legs feel too wobbly to stand. I throw my head between my legs just in time. Just like Dr. Judy told me to.

Inhale: one, two, three, four, five. Exhale: six, seven, eight, nine, ten. Everything is OK. I open my eyes, but everything's still splotchy, so I repeat the breathing sequence, eyes shut tight again.'

Something's welling up. But the tears don't come. I'm not crying. I'm never crying. I should be crying. But they don't come, not now, not the last time I was here. Not even the first time I ever stepped foot in St. Christopher's, with Dad, last spring.

•   •   •

It was a Saturday afternoon in May, and Dad and I had just gone to a photography exhibit at the Train Station. Mom was in New York visiting her younger sister, Aunt Emmy. The Train Station hadn't been a train station for decades; it had been restored and turned into an event space and art gallery. The exhibit was for a photographer, David Westerly, this guy Dad went to Tisch with. At NYU.

Westerly's pretty famous now and most of the pictures in the exhibit were black and white portraits of regular people. They were cool. You saw the photos and you just knew life had slapped these people around. But it hadn't beat them. They were still fighting. That's what I liked about them—the defiance in each one of his subjects.

Dad pointed out how good David was, the way he positioned the light to always hit their faces, to illuminate all the expression lines. And how he always employed the rule of thirds—that photographs turn out better with subjects off-center.

"Was that hard for you?" I asked as we walked back to the car.

"Hard? Enjoying photography with my daughter? You kidding me?" he said, and he squeezed me into him, the way he did, where I felt like I was the world's most special person.

"Your pictures are as good as David Westerly's," I said, getting into the car.

"You think so?" He rubbed his chin. "Maybe. The problem is it's hard to get known like that up here."

"If you're not in New York City."

"Right."

"Do you ever wish you and Mom had stayed?"

He looked over at me, then returned to the road. "Oh honey," he said, and he was quiet for a moment. Then he shook his head. "I wouldn't change anything."

Afterward, we went to get ice cream at Scoops. I offered to pay, since I get an employee discount—at least, I did at that point. They were out of Tiger Tail (my go-to), so I got Chocolate Fudge Swirl instead.

Dad ordered Pralines 'n' Cream. We were almost done our cones when Dad put his down on the table and leaned over the edge of his chair, holding his stomach.

"Dad? Dad?"

"Dad, what's wrong?"

I went behind the counter to get a glass of water.

My dad just shook his head when I set it down in front of him. The sound of his breathing had changed. There was a raspy quality to it. He struggled up to stand, until he was hunched over, and he leaned on me as we walked out to the car. "Dad, you're kind of scaring me."

His face was gray. "I"—A smear of ice cream was still on his chin. He wiped it off. "I'm—it's never been this bad."

It took him ages to dig his keys out of his pocket, then he passed them to me. I had my learner's but I'd only practiced, like, five times. All with Dad. We were 10 blocks from our house. I could do that. This was just another practice session. But halfway there, Dad told me to turn left, and then right. I asked him where we were going, but he wouldn't say, until we turned right on Elm. The hospital was straight ahead, through the intersection. Dad had one hand on his stomach and reached over to put the other on my shoulder.

"You're doing great, honey," he said.

The parking job I did was the world's worst—we'd never worked on parking before. By the time the car stopped, my dad was breathing normally. "Ooh," he said. "Dr. Morgenstern is going to be pissed."

Morgenstern was the name on the sign by the

curb. I pictured this stuffy doctor rolling up in a Mercedes-Benz and confronting our broken-down Honda in his place and actually giggled. Then my dad's breathing changed. He winced. Pulling him out of the car seemed impossible—but I did it. He leaned on me all the way in, insisting we go through the main doors, not the ER, and I agreed because it was less scary that way. The concrete stairs up to the main entrance seemed to go on forever, until finally the glass doors slid open, to swallow us whole.

● ● ●

"Hey, are you OK?"

There's a hand on my shoulder, startling me out of my thoughts. I open my eyes and focus, and nearly lose my breath again. It's him. Dylan McCuter. Excuse me, Dylan McCutter. Two t's. Small detail.

He's tall (but not too tall), thin (but muscular) and as he bends down, his caramel-colored hair falls forward. It's all brown with golden highlights from the summer. Stubble darkens his face and there's the dimple he gets in his left cheek when he smiles. He's wearing a long-sleeved gray jersey, dark jeans faded over the knees and gray Converse high-tops. And those green eyes . . .

His hand moves to my slightly sweaty panic-attack back as he sits down beside me on the steps. "Philadelphia Greene."

He. Knows. My. Real. Name.

I blink in disbelief. The only people who know my real name are in my classes, since they hear it when the teachers read out the attendance at the start of the term. But Dylan was two years ahead of me when I was a sophomore, so we never had any classes together.

"What are you doing out here?" he asks.

"Oh, um . . ."

What *am* I doing out here?

The volunteer meeting! Crap. I grab my phone from the front of my bag. It's already 5:15. I've taken my own future into my hands by missing more than half the meeting. They probably won't even *let* me volunteer now. Problem solved. Except . . .

"Are you a volunteer?" I ask. Maybe Dylan's the motivation I need to actually go through with this. I can do this. Sure, I had a panic attack just standing at the front doors, but so what? Maybe this huge building of nightmares isn't the, uh, huge building of nightmares that I think it is. Maybe it's about true love. I mean, helping people. I'm so lost in my own thoughts I miss what Dylan replies about being a volunteer.

"I think I've pretty much totally missed the volunteer meeting," I say to cover up. "Where are you headed?"

"Uh . . . was just playing music for the patients . . ."

"Are you a volunteer?" I risk asking again.

He shakes his head. "Not exactly. Me and a couple guys play music for some of the patients. So it's not, like, being a full-on volunteer."

Why couldn't I do that, instead of being a front-line candystriper? Oh, because I have zero musical talent, that's why. "Cool," I say.

Dylan's phone buzzes and he checks it. "I gotta split. You sure you're OK?"

I nod.

"All right then. So I guess I'll be seeing you around, Philadelphia Greene," Dylan says, standing up. He gives me a smile, his dimple disappearing under his stubble, and then he turns and walks down the steps.

I quickly grab my vintage Nikon from my bag, focus and snap a pic of him. Yeah, the best subjects get the film treatment.

The first thing I see when I wake up every morning are my dad's photos. For my 16th birthday, my dad gave me wallpaper. Weird gift, right? Before I saw it, when it was still all rolled up, I was like, Seriously? I ask for an iPhone and I get wallpaper? But then I unrolled it. He had taken hundreds of his photos— some of his favorites and my own, pics of me and him, my mom and him, all three of us together, and ones of he and my mom before I was born—and collaged them in black and white and then had it turned into wallpaper. We spent the weekend of my birthday wallpapering my room. Now, I see him right before I close my eyes, and as soon as I wake up. A constant.

I pull on my jeans and favorite hoodie—my dad's, light gray with purple lettering, from when he went to Tisch. It's only two years till I'll be going there too—at least, I hope so.

Mom's door is still closed and it's dark in her room so I tiptoe downstairs. Who knows what time she finally came home from work last night. She cares about the animals, sure, but she gets paid more to work overtime, and we need the money. In the kitchen I grab an apple from the bowl on the counter, pull on my broken-in black boots and slip out the front door. It's my favorite time of day to shoot, when there's just enough light, but the world isn't entirely awake.

I walk to the end of our street where there are usually signs for garage sales stapled to the wooden lamppost. I started shooting garage-sale finds this past summer. I like how random it can be: old typewriters with missing keys, or wooden chests that may have held love letters. I take a picture of the garage sale signs so I'll have the addresses stored, then turn right onto Waverly, left onto Calcutta and then left again onto Peabody, to the first sale. Within a few minutes, I can see there's a ton of old stuff—like they've lived in the house forever and are finally clearing out all the boxes in the basement they don't want to take with them. Vintage jars and records and dusty hardcover books. There's an old desk with a hole cut in its top. I look around and see a balding guy taking a sip of a coffee from a mug that's shaped like a football.

"Can I take some pics?" I ask, holding up my camera.

"Doesn't bother me. Stuff's just sitting here collecting dust anyway," he says, then nods at the desk.

"That's a sewing machine. My grandmother's. She had 17 kids, and she used to make all their clothes," he says. "We're moving my mother into a nursing home, so this stuff's got to go."

After taking a few pictures of the sewing table, I pay 50 cents for an old milk bottle that says *Bencher's* in half-scratched-off letters. I imagine it came from a milk delivery company ages ago, back when the blue-uniformed delivery guy used to leave the bottle on your doorstep every few days. In a few weeks this purple wildflower that I love will show up in the ravine, and I'll put some in the Bencher's bottle.

The next garage sale has tons of collections: records, stamps, baseball cards. There's a box of old photo albums. All the pictures have been removed, the white squares where they used to be visible against the yellowed paper. The acetate no longer sticks. I flip the pages and discover one photo left. It's a square picture, shot in black and white with a white border, from the '50s, maybe earlier. A young boy, two or three years old, stands in the middle of a snowy front yard at night, a streetlamp glowing overhead. He's holding a shovel that's taller than him, and I can barely see his face beneath the furry trim on the hood of his one-piece snowsuit. I lay the album down and take a close-up of the lone photo on the page, the crinkled acetate making the photo look even older than it is. It could work well for my Vantage Point theme: memories.

Then I spot it: *The Catcher in the Rye*. The cover is shiny silver, with black lettering at the top. I don't have this edition. It probably seems like a cliché, but *The Catcher in the Rye* is my favorite book. I thought I'd hate it when it was assigned last year in English class because the main character is a 17-year-old boy—and I didn't think I'd be able to relate—but Dad convinced me to give it a shot, telling me how much he loved it, how Holden goes to New York, and how he read it when he first moved to the city. Anyway, there's this part where Holden explains how, when he's worrying about something, he has to go to the bathroom, only he doesn't go, because he's too worried to go and doesn't want to interrupt his worrying to go. Like how I get with the panic attacks. Anyway, it's the last book Dad and I read together. Whenever I see a copy, I buy it.

After the third garage sale, I head home. We've lived in the same house at 42 Catalina Drive since I was three. It used to belong to Grandma Anne and Grandpa Frank, my mom's parents, but then they moved into a nursing home and gave the house to Mom and Dad, who didn't have the money to buy their own. It's a short walk from the Cherokee River, which runs through Spalding and connects all the little towns in the area. Most of Spalding's original houses (which were more like cottages) were torn down and replaced or renovated beyond recognition. But ours is still the original cottage. It's the only one on the street like it. I used to wish we had a big new house, like Dace's, but now I like that ours is different from all the others. Dark brick with faded gray wood trim amid houses with that plasticky siding or blah concrete look. Our house looks like a Swiss Alps chalet. The roof goes right down, almost to the ground, and the front windows have these big red wooden shutters.

Inside the house is quiet—the only sign of Mom is a note on the pad of lined yellow paper, on the kitchen counter.

Pipsqueak—
At clinic till 3. Got you appt w/ Dr. Judy at
1. Please go. Not convinced hospital placement
is good idea. Call me after you talk to her & let
me know what she says. Love you.

Mom

I tear the page off the pad, crumple it and toss it in the recycling under the sink. Little does she know *not* volunteering there may be the real problem, given how I missed the meeting and all.

"*Catcher in the Rye*," I say to Dad when I get to my room, focusing on the pic I usually do: he's 17, standing by the stoop of his apartment on Christopher Street in the West Village. Hands in the pockets of his jeans, camera around his neck.

The milk bottle just fits on my windowsill. I drag my desk chair over to the floor-to-ceiling bookshelf in the corner beside my desk and slip the book onto the top shelf, next to the other copies. This one makes eight.

Then in the bottom of my bag I find the paper — totally crumpled—with the volunteer coordinator's name on it, and punch the hospital number into my phone. Probably a futile attempt given it's Saturday, but I go through the 17 prompts until I'm connected to Glenys Grange. Shock of all shockers, she answers. Maybe the volunteer gods *are* on my side.

"Why weren't you at the candystriper orientation yesterday afternoon?" she asks, her voice high-pitched.

Oh that? I was busy having a panic attack. I consider confiding in her, thinking she might take pity on me, but who would want a volunteer who is likely to spontaneously collapse and have a freakout session in the middle of the hospital?

Instead, I tell her I had a small scheduling conflict, but that I'm ready to get going on being St. Christopher's best volunteer ever.

She makes a mmm-ing noise for longer than necessary and then rustles some papers for what seems like forever. "We already created the schedule and handed out the uniforms. I'll have to see if there are any left, and I can't promise there'll be one in your size. This *really* is a hassle . . ."

"Please?"

She sighs. "We've been understaffed since the layoffs last summer anyway, so I suppose we can use the extra help. Fine—you can start Monday after school. Just wear khakis, a white shirt and non-marking soled shoes. I'll put you on for Mondays and Tuesdays."

"Oh well, um . . ."

"Is there a problem?" Glenys puffs.

I want to ask what day the music team works. Dylan works Fridays. What's the point of volunteering if I'm on totally opposite to Dylan? That's the whole *point* of volunteering. Oh, and getting in my mandatory-to-graduate hours. And helping people.

"No. I just would love to work Fridays," I say.

"Fine. Mondays, Tuesdays and Fridays. Be here at 3:30, sharp."

What? Three days instead of two? That was *not* in the plan.

• • •

Dr. Judy's is nothing like what I pictured a shrink's office would be like before I started coming to see her three months ago. She's not a psychiatrist, she's a psychologist, which is supposed to be more about talking through your feelings and less about popping pills and masking your feelings. But you'd think that the space would be more conducive for blathering on and on, more like what you see in the movies or on TV shows: mahogany paneling, dark carpeting, a massive couch that you can stretch out on with your head on one arm rest and your feet not even touching the other side. And the tables would have Tiffany lamps or those banker lights that give a yellow glow, and the psychologist would sit in a high-backed leather chair that swivels, taking notes on a yellow steno pad.

Yeah, well. Dr. Judy's office is the exact opposite. The waiting room is all white walls and hard plastic white chairs. Even the coffee table is bare—not even a magazine. It looks like she just moved in, but apparently she's been here for years, which sort of makes it seem like she's running a front for a drug-smuggling operation or the Mafia. But she hasn't been busted yet, so it's probably unlikely.

Inside her office, the furniture is super modern and super uncomfortable. There's no couch, but instead those wide pleather chairs that slope backwards so you either have to perch uncomfortably on the edge, or sink back into it and let your feet come off the floor, so it's like you're trapped in the chair. It's the worst.

And even though the walls are lined with bookcases, they're white, just like the walls, and they're totally empty except for three books. Seriously, rows and rows of bookshelves, and only three books, leaning up against each other in one of the shelves in the middle. They're some sort of psychology books, but three books that barely fill one of the cubbyholes, and the other 11 empty? It's bizarre.

Dr. Judy is also totally atypical. Not at all warm and fuzzy in wool sweaters and corduroy skirts. Her go-to outfit is a black suit with a colored silk shirt underneath. Pink, purple, teal, coral—I've seen them all. Black pumps, black stockings. And hair pulled back in a tight bun. Instead of a steno pad, she types on her laptop. She says it helps her keep all her notes easily filed, but it's really quite distracting because when I'm talking, I feel like it should be quiet and soothing. But instead, she's clacking away. I bet she's online shopping.

I take a sip of water, moving the glass from the table with the box of tissue to the floor beside me and wait for her to say something. Eventually she looks up.

"Do you think this is a good idea?"

"It's fine," I say, making eye contact. "I just finished sorting everything out with the coordinator. Besides, a guy I like is also volunteering. It's going to be totally distracting."

Dr. Judy slides her glasses onto her forehead and studies me. Why did I have to say that word? Dr. Judy hates distractions. She says distractions are an avoidance technique. And she hates avoidance worse than she hates distractions.

"Not distracting. Just fun, I mean. You know, like a normal teenager?"

"When do you start?" She takes a sip of coffee and wipes off the mark the cup left on her desk.

"Monday after school."

"How long is the shift?"

I tell her I'm not sure.

"Well, try to keep it short." Instead of telling me to leave if I feel uncomfortable, she says to stick it out for the entire shift. "Remember your coping techniques. And I see you . . . Wednesday, right?" She looks back at her computer. "So we'll check in then." I wonder if she'll charge the full amount for this 15-minute squeeze-in between her Saturday regulars. "Good luck, Pippa," she says. "I think this might turn out to be good for you."

● ● ●

"Funeral Boy," Dace says dramatically, twisting her Oreo apart then licking the filling. I dip my own cookie—still intact—into my glass of Diet Coke. Disgusting to some, I know, but I like the way the bubbles make the cookie tingle in my mouth. It's Sleepover Saturday.

We're in Dace's room, spread out on her bed: feet on the pillows, heads at the end of the bed, our stash of Oreos, Twizzlers and bottles of Diet Coke (for me) and water (for Dace) strewn across the white carpet. *Say Anything* is playing on the flatscreen on the wall in front of us, muted. It's about a cute slacker guy who loves a girl who's valedictorian. Dace's bedroom looks like the cover of Coconut Records' *Nighttiming* (which is no coincidence; she emailed her mom the cover art and told her that's what she wanted for her sweet 16). Pretty much everything is creamy white— desk, dresser, carpeting, even her door, which has a full-length mirror on the back. The exceptions are these super cool pink curtains behind her bed that make it look like there's a window there, only there isn't. (On the album cover, there's a massive eyeball peeking through the curtains, but Dace's mom vetoed that part.) On her side tables—which are made of stacked bricks—are these really cool vintage-y lamps with yellow shades. It's magazine-perfect, a.k.a. the total opposite of my room, which is sort of organized chaos.

I just told her about my encounter with Dylan. I thought she'd think I was being pathetic—Dace tends to treat her crushes like her contact lenses: two weeks and she tosses them. But I've been into Dylan ever since I first met him—in freshman year. It wasn't the ideal scenario: I was mid-freakout at 9:05 on the third day of school. I couldn't get my locker to open even though I'd tried, like, 42 times. And I couldn't just go to first period without my books because I'd oh-so-brilliantly taped my timetable to the inside of my locker door. I couldn't remember where first period was. Great plan, huh? So I was in the middle of freaking out (this was the pre–panic attack era) when Dylan swooped in, banged on my locker a few times and magically opened it.

"No problem," he said, as I fell in love with him. "Happens all the time."

I'd sometimes see him in the hall after that. He'd nod or smile. But nothing more. Since he was a junior we never had any reason to talk. Other girls would've made up an excuse: thrown a party, or straight-up asked him out, or even—cheesy as it is—sent him a candygram on Valentine's Day, but I couldn't bring myself to do any of those things.

Then last spring the paper decided to run a feature on what colleges the seniors had picked, and I got the story. I asked him to be in the story, and we talked for a while about the admissions process and how hard it was to get into Harvard. And since I'd never really forgiven myself for not asking him out over the past two years, I asked him one last question: who are you taking to prom?

You know, purely for professional reasons. For the story. There was a long pause while he looked at me. Or, rather, the camera lens I was hiding behind. And I snapped my favorite picture of him. It's in my nightstand drawer. He's looking directly into the camera. Like he's looking for something. In the moment, I got a feeling like a rollercoaster drop.

Was he . . . ? Then he shrugged. Said he'd probably go, but he wasn't going to bring a date just for the sake of bringing someone.

And then I forgot all about Dylan for a while. About everything, really.

"Of all the boys in all the volunteer placements, you get Funeral Boy," Dace says, licking the middle of her cookie.

"I wish you wouldn't call him that," I say, leaning over the end of the bed to dunk another Oreo in my glass of Diet Coke. "It makes him sound like he's going to die or something."

"It's a term of endearment," Dace says, popping up onto her knees and throwing one of her cookie wafers at the trash can. She sinks it and raises her arms in victory, then concentrates on the other half. She had been on the school basketball team since middle school, but this year she didn't even try out. So she could focus on modeling. "But listen, are you sure you can handle it?"

"Dylan?" I say.

"The hospital."

I nod. "Totally. That's what therapy's for, right?" I grab my camera off the floor beside the bed and shoot Dace for a while. She stands up, hands on hips, and studies me, the lens between us.

"Honesty Pact?" She grabs a Twizzler from the bag on the floor, her long blonde hair falling over her shoulders and partly covering her face. As she stands up she flips her hair back and bites off a piece, twirling the remainder in the air.

"Honesty Pact," I reply.

"OK, then let's get down to real business," she says. "How you're going to be spending all your waking hours with the boy you love."

"Not all my waking hours. Three afternoons a week. *If* he's even there those days. And I don't love him."

"Bullshitake mushroom."

I lower my camera. "OK, maybe I used to have a crush on him, but that's over. Remember the gay theory?"

"Yes. No. We had a gay theory?" She grabs a lip-gloss from the top of her dresser, then studies herself in the mirror as she applies it.

"Mmm-hmm. He's never dated a girl," I remind her.

"Not that we know of. And it's not like we've seen him with any guys."

"True." I put the camera down on the bed.

"Maybe he just has really high standards." Dace climbs back onto the bed.

"Spalding had a lot of pretty seniors last year."

"It's not just about looks," Dace says. "You know that."

"OK, consider the gay theory set aside for the moment. But there's no evidence he likes me. Or thinks of me at all."

"False, *Philadelphia*. And there's no evidence that he doesn't."

Dace grabs the remote off her nightstand and points it at the TV, pausing it. The main guy is standing in the front yard of a house, holding over his head—what, exactly?

"What's he holding up?" I squint at the TV.

"Seriously the biggest radio I've ever seen. How can he even hold it over his head?"

"Who cares? He's got the right idea. You need a grand gesture. Like this dude. You've got to take a chance and see what happens. Or you'll never know. This is your last chance. Isn't he going away to college? God, your life *is* this movie."

"Yeah, that's sort of a problem . . ." I say. "It's three weeks into the term. He should *be* at Harvard. Why isn't he there?"

"Maybe he's commuting."

"From Spalding to Boston every day? That's only, like, seven hours. No biggie."

"Sorry, I didn't realize this was geography class," Dace says, stabbing me in the arm with the remote. "Maybe he's home for the weekend. To volunteer at the hospital. Who cares? Point is, I'd say you got the best volunteer placement of all."

The hospital is about a half hour walk from school, but there's a path at the end of the football field that leads to the ravine, and you can walk the entire way there, totally oblivious to the rest of the world. It's like a hidden forest—even when it's bright out, it's a dark and ominous world in the ravine, as though it's the land the sun forgot. Once I'm down there, I look through my camera up at the canopy the red oak trees create. I adjust the aperture as high as it can go and then zoom in on a branch right above my head, bringing it into focus and letting the leaves go out of focus. It's one of my favorite techniques—there's nothing special about this particular branch in the ravine. But focusing on something so specific, and letting everything else go, gives me a sense of calm.

The path exits onto an easement between two

houses, and then it's a short walk to the end of a residential street, through the parking lot of a plaza and then around the back of the hospital to the front door. Climbing the stairs, I take a deep breath. On the top step I point my camera down and snap a picture of just the toes of my sneakers in the bottom third of the lens. And breathe.

This time I make it past the front door unaccompanied by my best bud, Mr. Panic Attack. Dark gray speckled floors, light gray walls lined with plaques of donators' names, a large fountain in the middle of the atrium, the elevators beyond. The reception desk is to the right, but it's empty. An elevator is waiting, doors ajar. The doors close behind me, then reopen on the fourth floor. Fluorescent lighting illuminates a world tinged in yellow—the walls, the tile floor, even the vinyl chairs in the small waiting room I pass. The nurses' station is to the left, and one of three wipe boards on the wall has *CANDYSTRIPERS* written in black marker across the top. Someone's added an extra "P" with a blue pen and an arrow. I've got to remember to tell Dace about that later.

"You're late." A girl glares at me. She's got to be five years older than me, with enviable zit-free, buttery skin and blue eyes. She'd be really pretty if it weren't for her massive frown. Her blonde hair is pulled tightly into a bun. She's wearing a super cute pink-and-white striped polo shirt, khakis and a pair of Crocs. Unfortunate, that last bit. Her name tag says *Hannah*.

"Where have you been?" She shakes her head.

"Honestly, why are there always a million of you kids in every other ward except mine?"

I shove my camera in my bag and stash it under the counter with the other bags.

"I need you on—" she checks her clipboard "—plant watering." She grabs a watering can off one of the shelves and thrusts it at me. "Do the entire rehab ward, and come find me when you're done."

Water plants. Easy. How could I screw that up?

"Oh, and what's your name?"

"Pippa."

"Spell it."

I watch her scribble my name on her clipboard as I spell it.

"Don't take too long. I have about a million things I need you to do."

How many plants are in the ward? Where *is* the rehab ward? And how am I going to sneak away and figure out where the music team plays?

A directory points me in the right direction— to both the rehab ward and the bathroom, where I fill up the watering can. Then I knock on the first door in the hall. There's no answer, and the room is empty. No patients, no plants.

Easy peasy.

In the next room there's a woman lying in the bed, her eyes closed.

"I'm just here to water your plants," I tell her in my most professional voice. She doesn't open her eyes. Her hair is long and white and fanned out over her pillow. I'm just thinking how pretty her hair looks and how I should consider having long hair like that when I'm old when my heart starts beating really quickly and the walls seem like they're really close and my throat feels like there are cotton balls in it and I can't breathe out my nose either because there are cotton balls in there too. I rush into the hall and drop the watering can, then fall to my knees. I push myself against the wall, sit on my bum and lock my head between my knees. The watering can is on its side, spilling the water.

Inhale, count to five, exhale, count to 10.

Then I do the technique of talking myself through the situation, like Dr. Judy taught me.

Me: "Why are you feeling weird?"

Also Me: "The lady in the bed."

Me: "What about her?"

Also Me: "She didn't look like she was breathing."

Me: "Good. You've identified the source of your anxiety."

Also Me: "What's good about that? How am I going to volunteer if I keep freaking out like this?"

Me: "Focus on the present. Focus on the facts. That woman was just sleeping."

Also Me: "I know."

Me: "Lots of people get better in the hospital."

Also Me: "I know."

I say "I know" a few more times, breathing in on one word and out on the next, the way Dr. Judy told me to. Then I lift my head up and open my eyes.

OK, Pippa. The first time you entered a hospital room with an actual patient inside? You know, since the last time you entered a hospital room?

You failed.

• • •

It takes me awhile to clean up the spill in the hall with paper towels from the bathroom, but I finally get it dry and then refill the watering can and get back out into the hall. Dr. Judy says that the best thing to do when I'm in an uncomfortable situation is to stick it out and push through. Giving in to my anxiety and running from the situation makes it even harder to come back. So let's try this again.

In the next room there's an elderly woman (awake, thankfully) sitting at the end of her bed, holding lipstick in one hand and a small compact mirror in the other. She looks over at me. Bright green eyeshadow goes from her lash line up to her eyebrows. Blush smears from her nose to her ears.

"Oh hello!" she says as she looks up from the compact. "What do you think of this shade?"

She purses her lips. The lipstick dyes her lips, yep, as well as a swath of the rest of her face. Maybe I debate what to say for a moment too long.

"You hate it. Too dark? Too red?"

"No. Well, it's just that, it's a bit overpowering for your skin tone," I say, then regret my honesty. Who am I to judge?

She frowns at her reflection. "Maybe you're right." She sighs. "I just wanted to look nice."

"Oh you do look nice!" I'm not being a very helpful or friendly candystriper. "Are you expecting someone?"

"No. But doing my makeup makes me feel better, especially when I'm cooped up in here. I only just got around to it now, though, and the day's half over."

The windowsill has a lineup of vases. The first holds daisies and is filled halfway with water. Am I supposed to top up the vase? Hannah didn't mention anything about cut flowers in vases. I decide to go for it, then move on to the spider plant beside it. Then some other plant with large green and white leaves.

"You forgot the one on the end."

I eye the pink plant at the end of the row. "Isn't that a cactus?" I say, unsure.

"Ha! I like you. You're the first girl who's known that in the two months I've been here. The others all fall for my little test and water it."

Two months? She doesn't really look sick, but why else would she be here so long? Unless she's never coming out of the hospital. I push that thought away.

"You know what *does* need water?" she sing-songs, snapping the compact shut and putting it on the tray table with her lipstick.

I shake my head.

"Dorothy."

Oh great, she names her plants. "Which one's Dorothy?"

She gives a deep, throaty chortle and points at herself.

"Oh," I say, then laugh.

"I'm so thirsty and all they give us to drink are these tiny cups of water." She points at the paper Dixie cup by her bed. "I'd love to get a glass of fizzy water. With those bubbles that make you burp but feel *so* good in your mouth?" She grabs a tattered fabric change purse from beside her bed and opens it, then hands me a five-dollar bill.

"Like Perrier?"

Dorothy nods. "That would be really lovely, dear."

I smile. "Sure thing. I'll be back in a minute."

At the nurses' station, I grab my bag from under the desk and head to the elevator, happy for the break. I've been watering plants for what . . . an hour? I check my watch. Oh. Twenty minutes. Well, whatever.

I push the elevator button just as I hear a familiar voice behind me. "Now where do you think you're going?"

My stomach lurches and I turn around to see Hannah. This is like *Silence of the Candystripers*, and Hannah-ble Lecter is going to bite off my tongue.

"I—I'm just going to the cafeteria to—"

"Cafeteria? You work five seconds and you're already taking a break?" As the doors to the elevator open, she waves the trio of doctors inside to go on without me. "We've got a Code Yellow. Room 414."

"Code Yellow?" I look around. I'm guessing she's not referring to the décor fail in this joint.

She shoves a set of folded white bedsheets and a bottle of disinfectant at me, then heads back to the nurses' station.

I shuffle down the hall to room 414 and push open the door. A burst of urine-infused air hits me in the face.

The clean sheets end up on the green vinyl chair in the corner so I can grab a tissue from the box beside the bed. I tear it in half then twist each into tight rolls, kind of like Twizzlers, and stuff them up my nose. Test inhale. Can't smell a thing. Perfect. Or, as close to perfect as you can get when you're about to change soiled sheets.

There's a dispenser on the wall for plastic gloves. With my hands all latexed up I'm ready to conquer the bed. It's not the wetness of the sheets that makes them disgusting—well, it is, but it's also the fact that they're still warm. I put them in the bin marked *soiled linens* outside the door and toss out my gloves. Hopefully the most disgusting task I'll ever have to do here.

The nurses' station looms at the end of the hall, but Hannah's not there. Score. Down on the first floor cafeteria I grab a Perrier for Dorothy, two Diet Cokes—if the Code Yellow's any indication, it seems like a two DC kind of afternoon. Oh, and a bag of Twizzlers from the bottom shelf of the candy display. As I'm standing up, I nearly hit my head on a guitar. That's attached to a boy. Dylan.

"Hey," he says, and his hair falls over his eyes. I drop everything. Literally. Plastic bottles everywhere.

We both bend over to pick them up. "Thirsty?" he asks as he hands me the Perrier.

"Diet Coke?" I ask, handing him mine. Nice gesture, except I haven't even paid for it yet. "I mean, I'll pay for it."

"Oh thanks, but I don't drink aspartame," he says. He rubs his nose.

Which makes me rub *my* nose. And that's when I

realize the tissues are still up there. Twizzler style. I yank them out of my nose.

"I was just changing the sheets," I say, flustered. "Code Yellow?"

He gives me a blank look.

"You don't know Code Yellow?"

"No, I . . ." he starts to say.

"Oh yeah, music team. I forgot. So lucky."

He nods. "Right. So what's a Code Yellow?"

"You don't want to know."

He raises his eyebrows. "As in . . . really?"

"Number one. The tissues were to block the smell." We move into the checkout line.

"Interesting tactic. Did it work?"

"Kind of. But the embarrassment factor might be worse than smelling someone else's urine."

"Just be glad it wasn't a Code Brown."

"Code Br—" I shake my head. "No way. Is there such a thing?"

He shrugs. "Guess you'll find out." He looks me up and down. "Cute uniform."

"Hey Dyl." Dylan turns and I follow his gaze to the cashier, who's looking over at us. Let's be real. She's not looking at me at all. She's totally focused on Dylan. Dyl, actually. DYL? Why is she calling him DYL? Ugh.

"Oh hey Callie," he says, giving her a little punch on the arm.

Greaaaaaaat. He knows her name. And she gets skin-to-skin touching.

I study her, as she flips her long black hair over

her shoulder. Even though she's wearing a green apron she has on a low-cut white tank, and her perky boobs and tiny waist just kind of announce themselves. It's like, Hi! Here we are!

Why can't I look like that in my uniform?

"How are you?" she asks *Dyl*, putting her hand on his.

Dylan looks at me and then back at her. "Great, thanks," he says. "Just great. Grabbing a drink."

"The usual?" she says, as he puts a bottle of cranberry juice on the counter. He has a usual and she knows what it is?

I open my mouth to say something—anything— but no sound comes out. I try again but end up making a weird half-cough noise.

"Oops, sorry. You go ahead of me. You've got a lot of drinks to deliver, and I don't want to hold you up," he says.

Ugh. Why did I have to buy so many drinks? I try to do a nice thing and it totally backfires on my love life. "Oh, that's OK. You're not holding me up."

"Well you're kinda holding the *line* up," Callie interjects, giving me one of those annoyed, fake smiles, and Dylan laughs, as though she's made a joke, but she really doesn't look like she's kidding. Dylan hands her a five for his cranberry juice.

"It's on me, Dyl," Callie says, refusing to take the bill. "I owe you from Friday night."

Friday night?

"So what do you think about Callie? Do I need to worry?" I ask Dace as I toss my bag in my locker and pull out my books for first period.

Our lockers are in the main hallway—and it's no fluke they're side by side. It took three days and seven chocolate bars to get Hanif Jaffer to trade me lockers. Hanif's a sophomore, and he loves Dace. But not more than he loves Kit Kats.

"Cafeteria Callie," Dace says sympathetically, clucking her tongue. She grabs a tube of Kiehl's lipgloss from the organizer on the top shelf of her locker and stuffs it in her pocket. "Gorgeous black hair? Curvy in all the right places? Good nail beds?"

"Yes, yes and really? I hadn't noticed."

Dace shrugs. "I always notice nice nails." She inspects her own for a moment, then snaps her fingers. "Callie Garcia. You know Breanne with the glasses, on the basketball team? Callie's her older sister. She graduated the year before we started. Yeah, she's hot."

"That *really* makes me feel better."

"Who cares if she's hot? He has good taste. And you know he's not gay."

"Part of me would rather he was gay than straight and not like me."

"That's ridiculous. As long as he likes girls, you have a chance. And who cares if she's his girlfriend? That's nothing that can't be changed."

"Oh no. Remember the rule about stealing boyfriends?"

THE RULE ABOUT STEALING
BOYFRIENDS
1. Don't.

"That's your rule, not mine," Dace says, fixing her hair in her locker mirror. "And anyway, this isn't at all like last time."

Oh, the last time. Thanks for bringing that up, Dace. So my only (sort of) real boyfriend so far was Reggie Stevenson in freshman year. Oh, Reggie, with his Brillo-pad hair that looked super cute but was super scratchy whenever his head rubbed against my face. He had a lot of zits but he also had a lot of freckles so they all just blended together and I really didn't care because he was so awesome. He would put little notes in my locker between classes and call me before he went to sleep and, OK, also I just really wanted a boyfriend. I actually thought we might be together forever, things were going so well, even if they didn't start out in the most ethical of ways.

Reggie Stevenson was Mariella Rocca's boyfriend. They'd already been going out before they even started at Spalding. But then, in the middle of freshman year, she got to do an exchange in Italy for the winter term and Reggie came into Scoops the day after she left, which was the day after Christmas. Which Dace said was so obviously a sign. Because no one had been in Scoops all week. Because it was DECEMBER and freezing and no one wanted ice cream. He came in every single day over the break, and by New Year's Eve, we were making out in the freezer. I felt totally guilty until he told me he broke up with Mariella and he asked me to be his girlfriend instead. Dace convinced me Mariella was probably off making out with the Justin Bieber of Italy and was all like, "Reggie who?" For months it was all butterflies and unicorns. I even believed Reggie when he said the reason he wanted us to keep our relationship a secret was because it gave us a special bond that no one could break.

We almost *did it*. I wanted to wait until March— three-month rule—but we never lasted that long.

Because guess what?

Turned out Reggie never broke up with Mariella. It was all a big fat lie. On the first day back after spring break—after he spent the whole week making out with me not only in the walk-in freezer at Scoops but also in my bedroom and his—there she was, back from Italia, and he went right back to being her boyfriend and it was like there had never been anything between us at all. And because I'd been a fool and believed that crap about our "special bond" no one but Dace knew we'd hooked up. So even if I'd tried to tell Mariella that she was dating a slime-ass, she probably wouldn't have believed me. And I didn't want to be *that* girl or make it look like I in any way wanted him back. Because I certainly did not. All I can say is that three-month rule really saved my butt. Or, more accurately, my virginity. And also, another reason I'm glad I quit working at Scoops at the start of last summer and am never going back.

Still . . . it was totally humiliating. But now that I'm over it, I'm glad the whole thing happened because I'm a lot less gullible.

Dace shuts her locker and leans against it. "So bottom line: you think Callie is his girlfriend because he punched her in the arm? Did I miss the status update on how punching someone in the arm means you want to get in their pants?" She punches me in the arm and grins.

"So you think it's nothing?"

"It's nothing. I've kissed guys who weren't my boyfriend and it's meant nothing. A punch in the arm is about as romantic as coughing at someone."

"Well, I wish he would've coughed at me."

"Oh you'll get your germs soon enough, my friend. And if by chance it's something more, who cares? In fact, we *want* Callie to be his girlfriend."

"We do?" I say as Emma passes us on her way to her locker, three down from Dace's.

"Cute warmers," I say. Emma always wears leg-warmers to school, which is the easiest way to tell her apart from her identical twin sister, Gemma. When it's warm, like today, she just wears them over bare legs. Today's are mint green and purple striped.

"Girlfriend is too strong a word. But maybe a girl that he's interested in. Or *thinks* he's interested in, until of course, you prove to him you're the one. Listen, Callie's probably more into Dylan than he is into her. So what you have to do is kill her with kindness. You know the saying: keep your friends close, and your enemies closer."

The *last* thing I want to do is have to fake niceties to someone I can't stand. It's so not me. And Dace knows it. I offer her a pained look, just to drive home the point.

"Sometimes we have to do things we don't want to do for the ones we love," Dace declares, then tells me she'll see me in History. I ask Emma if she's ready to go. We're in homeroom together.

Emma lets out a huge sigh and slams her locker. "I can't find my iPod."

"Maybe you left it at home?" She shakes her head as Ben passes us. He glances over, notices me and gives me a wink.

"We're on for lunch, right?" he asks, as though we have a date, and not a photo club meeting with four other members. Still, I feel myself blushing as I nod.

He keeps walking and I turn back to Emma, who's staring at me. "What was *that* all about?"

I just smile.

Can I see your shots?" Ben asks. I'm sitting in the photocopy room next to him at lunch, waiting for the photo club meeting to start. I hand over my camera. He studies one of my recent pics of Dace: she's in her bedroom getting ready to go out. I love the way the late afternoon sun hits her hair, making it look like ribbons cascading over her bare shoulders.

"Is that in sepia?"

"Yeah, I shot it that way. Shoot don't 'Shop," I add, then blush. Total nerd moment.

"Is that your motto?" he teases. He pulls his chair over so he's inches away from me and looks me right in the face with his big blue eyes.

"I know, it's kind of lame, but I'd rather get it right when I'm shooting than have to manipulate the image in post to get what I want."

"A girl after my own heart."

"Really?" I'm surprised. "Not many people feel that way. Especially now that it's so easy to alter them after. Like on Instagram. Everyone's a photographer."

"You're not on Instagram?" he asks in disbelief.

"Yeah I am, all I mean is . . ." I trail off.

Gemma rushes in, her tight black curls springing up and down, followed by Brooke, a sophomore who joined the club this year. We get started showing photos for this week's theme. Arlan goes first, since he chose the theme—Gray—and I follow next, plugging my flash drive into the computer that's connected to the projector and bringing up the photos. I'm pretty pleased because all three are gray naturally—not just shot in black-and-white, which I think is sort of taking the easy way out. First up is the album page at the garage sale, then my gray Tisch sweatshirt, tossed over the back of my white desk chair. The final one is from a rainy day last week. I'd framed the shot to capture the horizon where the gray sky met the river, my white bedroom window frame creating a border around a single oak tree. The entire shot is in shades of gray, giving it depth and nuance.

Jeffrey has a shot of a mitten (big surprise) but it's lying in the middle of an asphalt street. He shot in color but the result is entirely gray and really works. Gemma's photos are all shot in black-and-white. I tell her I like the shot of her white Pomeranian sitting on the couch, and suggest that if she'd found a gray blanket as a backdrop she could've shot in color for a stronger effect. We discuss whether shooting in black-and-white is really capturing gray as a theme, or if it's manipulating the theme.

Ben pipes in to agree with me, saying that we should be using our eye, not technology.

"Yeah but if you're purposely looking for shots that are gray, you're manipulating what could otherwise be a great shot, before you even take the picture," Jeffrey argues, despite the fact that two of his three shots are true gray shots.

"Sounds like you're being defensive," Ben retorts.

"Why don't you go next?" Jeffrey challenges him.

I'm about to say that Ben doesn't have to go if he's not prepared, but he stands up and plugs his iPad into the computer.

"Let's see . . ." He opens a folder labeled *Gray*, then starts his slideshow of more than a dozen photos.

The first is a guy sitting on a bench outside a rundown old gas station. Then a single white orchid blossom against a gray sky. A gray shower curtain in a white shower. Gray boots at a front door. A street scene with one light burnt out amid a row of glowing lampposts.

They're *good.* He totally has an eye for both angles and details. This is just what I need—he'll push me to be better. Except, the last thing I need right now is more competition for Vantage Point. Only the top two spots in each region go to Tisch Camp.

"Where'd you take the pic of the old guy?" Jeffrey asks Ben.

Ben shrugs. "My dad and I took a road trip last summer. Somewhere on Route 66. Don't remember which crappy little town. They all blended together after a while."

"And the lamppost? That looks familiar."

"A burnt-out lamppost looks familiar?" Ben laughs. "Dude, relax."

I ask if anyone has a suggestion for next week's theme, Ben's pictures still flittering through my internal viewfinder.

"What about groups of three?" Ben pipes up.

"When you say three, do you mean three, or do you mean 17 or 12 or 82?" Jeffrey grumbles.

The rest of us agree to the theme being Threes

and as the meeting breaks up, Ben approaches with a sly smile. "Want to shoot together till the bell rings?" My stomach flips—does that qualify as being asked out?

• • •

"Glenys wants to see you," Hannah says as soon as she sees me. She's behind the nurses' station, stacking supply boxes onto a dolly.

"What? Why?"

"Her office is on the third floor," Hannah says.

"But do you know why?"

"Pippa, her office is on the third floor."

Code Greene! Busted? But for what? I haven't done anything wrong! I've only been here for one shift so far!

Right. There is *no* way I'm going to Glenys Grange's office. I'll just leave. I'll quit before I can be fired. I'll sneak out. I'll . . .

"Hey, hold up," Hannah says. "I need to take these boxes to the third floor and they won't all fit on the dolly. Carry these two?" She nods at the boxes remaining on the floor. I follow Hannah to the elevator.

"Put those on the counter," Hannah says when we've reached the third floor nurses' station. "And Glenys's office is that way." The nameplate on the door says *Glenys Grange, Volunteer Coordinator*.

I cross my fingers then knock on the door. It swings open.

Glenys Grange looks me up and down. She has

poufy gray hair, brown bushy eyebrows. Clear plastic glasses sit on top of her head like a headband. She's wearing a bright pink T-shirt that says *I'm So Hip I Needed a Replacement.* Maybe she has a sense of humor? Laugh lines furrow the skin around her eyes, but she's not smiling now. "You must be Philadelphia. It's so nice to meet you in person."

We do the usual adult-teenager meeting mumbo-jumbo. Shaking hands and all that. She gets a few points after I call her Ms. Grange and she tells me I can call her "Glenys."

"Want to grab a seat?" Glenys points to a chair beside her desk. "I just wanted to check in and see how things are going?" she says in her high-pitched voice.

"Really?" I say.

"Yes. Hannah said she saw you yesterday, sitting in the hallway with your head between your knees."

"Ah."

Busted.

Glenys's eyes are wide. "She was worried about you. Some people just can't handle hospitals, Philadelphia. So how are you doing?"

You know what? If another person asks me how I'm doing I'm going to—well, I don't know. Something. Something crazy.

A rustle of paper. Glenys is going over a file folder on her desk. My handwriting's on it—the form I had to fill out after my volunteer assessment. Then she scans a different paper, something with a Spalding High School crest on it. My school file?

Does it mention my panic attacks? My heart starts to pound faster. Deep breath.

"I'm fine," I say. "I'm great. I'm really enjoying working here. The people are really nice."

Well, Dylan McCutter is really nice.

"Philadelphia. Philadelphia Greene," says Glenys. "Have we met before?"

"I don't think so. You know, about that fainting thing?"

"So you *did* faint?"

"No. Well, yes, almost. But it was, I have this blood sugar thing?" Totally made up. "And I just needed a glass of orange juice. I was fine after a glass of orange juice."

"Philadelphia Greene," she says again. She slips the glasses down onto her nose and peers at me. "Of course," she says. "You're Evan's daughter."

I nod, and the question comes again: "How *are* you doing?" But this time with more warmth. And this time I just shrug. Pause. Neither of us says anything.

And then I tell her the honest truth—that everyone always asks me that, that I've heard the question asked with about a billion different intonations and interrogatory uplifts and each time the answer is the same: fine, I guess. "I mean, I miss him, but everyone seems to be thinking I should be doing worse than I am, but I'm not: I think I'm fine. Why can't everyone just accept that?"

"So brave," she says.

"You know what, Glenys? Can we not do this? Can we just avoid distilling me down into some noble inspirational soul just because I happen to be Evan Greene's daughter? I don't feel brave at all. I don't feel inspirational. In fact, you know what? I don't feel anything. Which my therapist and my mother and my guidance counselor and pretty much everyone else tells me is a real problem. So that's how I'm doing. I'm *not* doing."

Dead air as Glenys watches me. There's a slight tint to her glasses. Is *she* crying? I squint and move my head, to see her from a different angle. When she does finally speak, she doesn't directly respond to anything I've said. "Your dad came in here one day and sat in that chair you're sitting in," she said. "I knew his name, of course, it's one of those names that everyone in Spalding seems to know, but I'd never met him. You see, I also run the hospital's art therapy program. Your dad needed my permission for a project. He wanted to shoot the hospital. As kind of our in-house photographer. To document our stories. I told him yes, of course. We'd be honored."

This is the first I've heard of any of this. "Do you have any of the photos?"

She must hear the hope in my voice. Photos of my dad's I didn't know existed? His captured memories? And by extension, him? I ache to see them.

But Glenys shakes her head. "Oh honey," she says, and this time a tear does run down her cheek. "He never got the chance."

● ● ●

I get on the elevator in a daze, not realizing it's going down instead of up. The doors open on the ground floor to what sounds like live music. Just before the doors close, I slip through and follow the sound around into the atrium. There he is.

He's resting against the edge of a large fountain in the center of the atrium. Head down, strumming his guitar. Two other guys are playing with him, one on bass and another on keyboards. Dylan's wearing faded jeans and a blue plaid shirt. He taps his right foot in time to the beat. When he sings I recognize the lyrics to "The Problem with Me"—a song from Dylan's band days. Rules for Breaking the Rules won Battle of the Bands three years running— I was there every time. Reflexively I retrieve my camera from my bag. He's engrossed in the music and doesn't notice me shooting as he plays. When I move my focus to capture the audience I notice they're all teens. One guy, about my age, is hooked up to an IV, the tubes connecting him to a pole on wheels, like he's a string puppet. A girl beside him has a bandana over her head. Another girl is bald. Cancer patients, all of them. I grip my camera and swallow hard.

Dylan just stands there when the song ends. The bass player moves next to him and then the keyboardist comes up on the other side. They put their arms around each other and bow, and then Dylan's bandmates point at Dylan and the clapping gets more intense. Dylan smiles and whispers something to the other guys, who laugh. Once the clapping dies and everyone starts breaking off into little groups, heading off to wherever they're heading off to, Dylan catches sight of me. He smiles, slings his guitar over his back and approaches. My heart races.

"Philadelphia Greene," he says, and I smile. "You're going to have to pay for those photos."

The best I can muster is a nervous laugh.

"Are you on a break? Want to grab a bite?" he asks.

I have never wanted to do anything more in my life.

●　●　●

"That's one inedible food group," Dylan says as we pass the Jell-O. *Three* glass bowls of Jell-O—I pull up my camera and snap a few pics for this week's photo club.

"I have a theory about that," I say, letting my camera dangle around my neck so I can grab a tray by the hot food.

"A theory, huh?" he says with a gorgeous grin. He has dark stubble, like he hasn't shaved in days. He really could not be any hotter. "I'd like to hear this theory." He punches me lightly in the arm. Punch. In. The. Arm. Yessss . . . Dace doesn't know what she's talking about. Punch in the arm = total, uncontrollable physical attraction.

"Gravy?" the lady behind the counter asks. I shake my head and she hands me a cardboard boat of fries, which I cover with cheese sauce over at the condiments. Dylan gets a burger and asks if I want to share a cookie.

Answer: Obviously.

"Chocolate chunk or white chocolate maca-damia nut?"

"Chocolate. Always chocolate. I don't like nuts."

"Not into nuts. Duly noted," he says. We take our trays over to the cash just as Cafeteria Callie walks up to the till and hands a key to the girl. She takes the key and they swap places. Great timing, I think, but then I remember my mission: Operation Kill Callie with Kindness. I plaster a smile on my face.

"Ili Dyl," she coos, totally ignoring me.

"Callie, hi!" I practically scream with enthusiasm.

They both stare at me like I'm certifiably crazy.

"Chocolate milk?" Dylan asks me, opening the fridge door.

I nod. He grabs two containers and puts them on his tray. Which makes it our tray, doesn't it? Sharing a tray, Callie. Take that.

"Dylan and I are going to eat together. Want to join us?" I say, praying that my assumption that she's just come back from a break is accurate, and she won't be able to.

"I'm working. Aren't *you* supposed to be?" she looks right at me.

Dylan just laughs. "Everyone needs a break once in a while, right?" He's been volunteering here longer. He must know what we can get away with, right?

Then, on our way to our table, he says, "That was nice of you to invite Callie to join us."

"Well, she's your friend, right?" I say, but I'm secretly praying he'll say, *No, she's my cousin.*

Instead he nods. "Yeah. She's great."

Great. Ughhhhhhh.

There's an empty table by the window but Dylan says he knows a better place to sit. I follow him to the metal door at the cafeteria's far end. Dylan pushes it open, holding it for me.

"Where are we?" I ask, looking around. It's like we've entered a hidden world—it's a space about the size of a large swimming pool, with trees hiding the walls of the hospital, and a small pond in one corner.

Tall reeds, lily pads—it's that kind of pond. Goldfish swim through the clear water. "They'll have to take those guys out soon, when it gets too cold," he says as he sets the caf tray down on the concrete edge of the pond, then sits down. I do too. It's cold on my butt, but I don't really care.

"Cool, right? They finished this place at the end of the summer but no one really seems to know about it yet, so it's like a secret hideout. It's supposed to be a retreat for people who spend a lot of time here. Chemo patients, palliative care, that sort of thing."

Dad would have liked this spot.

"But won't it remind people stuck here that they're never getting out?" I wonder aloud, looking at the lone bench, nestled in the tall grasses.

Dylan tilts his head back away from me. "I don't think so. It sucks being at the hospital, but people are here to get better. And there's no reason it can't be inspiring and hopeful."

"Hopeful?" I blurt out. "You're outside, but you're still in the hospital. It's like jail. How many cancer patients even leave this place? Alive, I mean."

Dylan's face clouds over. "Do you really think that?"

I shrug. Neither of us says anything for a moment.

"OK, Very Important Question," he says, and my breath catches in my throat.

He holds up a packet. "Ketchup on your fries?" he says, then looks at my tray. "Wait, *what* is going on with your fries?"

I force a laugh. "Cheese sauce."

He looks like he's in pain. "But why?"

This time my laugh's for real. "Awesome sauce, really. And yes to the ketchup."

"Both?"

"It's like mac 'n' cheese. Seriously insanely awesome." He squirts ketchup on my fries.

"Oh, and an example of three things that work so well together. Three's the theme this week in photo club," I explain, snapping a pic of my fries, then shaking my head. "Tastes better than it looks. Try one."

"I think I can safely disagree without even trying one. It looks disgusting."

"It's the theory. But you have to try one first, before I explain."

He reluctantly picks up a soggy fry and puts it in his mouth. He's not even done chewing when he holds up his hands. "What is going on here?" He swallows, then shakes his head. "This may be the best fry I've ever had in my life."

I laugh.

"How did you know that these soggy-looking things would be so kick-ass?"

I pop one in my mouth, then explain my theory.

"So let me get this straight. If the food *looks* good, it'll taste bad. But if it looks bad, it's going to taste great?"

I nod. "It's a simple formula."

Dylan grabs the cookie from his tray. "This is totally going to bust your theory," he says. "Look at this thing. Perfectly round. Evenly distributed chips. It looks great. How can you screw up a chocolate chip cookie?"

I shake my head. "Perfectly round. Evenly distributed chips. Clearly made in a factory months ago."

He breaks off a piece, then takes a bite. And makes a face. "Astonishingly terrible. It sort of tastes like those pellets you get at the petting zoo— to feed the deer?"

"Oh you've tasted those?" I smile.

"You know what I mean. You're blowing my mind, Philadelphia Greene."

"It's just a cookie." My face is hot.

"But it isn't. I'm starting to get you, I think. You don't do things like anyone else. Am I right?"

"What about you? Not many guys in bands get accepted to Harvard." Or go through high school somehow managing to be one of the coolest guys in the school, *and* friends with everyone. Always volunteering to help out at lame assemblies to make them fun, or open freshmen's lockers without making fun.

His face clouds again. He shrugs. "I guess." Then he slaps his leg and says he has an idea. "Every time you taste something delicious that looks awful, I insist you take a picture and text it to me. To remind me that something I never would've ordered is, in fact, edible."

"That sounds like a plot to make me your guinea pig," I say, though there's not one part of me that minds being his guinea pig.

"I prefer 'personal taste-tester.' It's a prestigious role, and I'll do the same for you." He pulls out his iPhone. "What's your number?"

Oh yesssssss. I shiver with excitement.

"Are you cold?"

"No," I say, then wish I'd said yes because now he's going to think I'm just nervous or something. But he takes off his plaid shirt and passes it to me. Underneath he's wearing a Rules for Breaking the Rules T-shirt.

His shirt is warm and soft, like it's been washed a thousand times, and smells like musky soap and peppermint gum. He unlocks his phone then slowly says, "Philadelphia Greene," as he types my name. His fingers look rough, I guess from playing guitar. "OK, hit me."

As he's looking down I seize the opportunity to check out his arms, which are muscular and tanned, but then I notice the inside of his right arm. It's badly bruised. He catches me looking and glances down, then slaps his hand over his arm and laughs.

"What happened?"

"Guitar injury," he says. "Hazard of being in a band."

Then my phone buzzes. Dylan McCutter has just sent me a text.

Spalding's on high alert. OK, not really, but Lisa calls an emergency *Hall Pass* lunch meeting, even though it's only Wednesday, because there's a big story breaking and she wants us to get it into the next issue, which comes out next Friday. At least seven people have had things stolen in the past two weeks. But we, the self-sacrificing staff of *Hall Pass*, are prepared to swap our pens for magnifying glasses and get to the bottom of the case of the stolen items. I kid. Lisa and I seem to be the only ones who care.

"Who wants to help cover the story?" Lisa asks from her place at the head of the photocopy room table.

"Can't," says Abigail, a senior staff writer. "I've already got two stories and a profile on the new Phys Ed teacher."

"What's the story anyway? A list of stolen items? Do we have any leads?" Brendan asks.

"Not yet, but maybe we can figure out a pattern," Lisa says. "We could have a serial on our hands."

Brendan raises an eyebrow, skeptical. Poor Lisa watches too much *Dexter*. I decide to throw her a lifeline.

"Why don't we make it a Streeter spread? Take pics of everyone who's had something stolen, and include a funny quote that ties in with the lost item?" Jeffrey's going to want to take this on, for sure. A bunch of lost items? It's Vantage Point gold for him.

"Good idea. Pippa, you OK to take it on?" Lisa asks me. I look over to Jeffrey, who's lost in his computer.

"Jeffrey, you want to double-byline it?" I ask but he shakes his head.

"Still working on getting all the headshots of the cast of *Annie*. Streeters are your thing. You find the stuff, then maybe I'll be interested." He smirks at me—nothing like a little friendly competition.

Fine," I say, secretly happy to get the story for myself, even though I really don't need more on my plate. But I remember Emma searching for her iPod the other day: I want to help her out if I can.

Lisa hands me a sheet listing the students who've had stuff stolen. Even though she takes her job *way* too seriously, I'm excited about this story.

I head out the back doors to the football field to find Cameron "QB1" Jenkins. The football team is trying to win the all-region championship this season, so their two a-day practices have turned into three-a-days. I ask the coach if Cam can talk to me for five minutes and he waves him off the field.

"I'm doing a piece for the paper about everyone who's had stuff stolen," I say as Cam takes off his helmet, his curly black hair plastered to his head, soaked with sweat. "I heard that you lost something?" I say in my most professional voice, pen and mini Moleskine notebook at the ready.

PIPPA'S RULES FOR INVESTIGATING

1. Never feed the person you're interviewing any info that you could otherwise catch them in a lie about.*

Cam tells me he lost *hwthymonimufth*.

"Can you take your mouthguard out? I can't really understand you."

He spits his mouthguard, all slimy and disgusting, into his hand.

"My heart-rate monitor—out of my locker in the changeroom. Coach makes me wear it because I get really riled up you know, and he doesn't want me to have a heart attack or whatever."

"Probably good advice," I say, taking notes, then slipping my notebook into my back pocket and tucking my pen back into my topknot. I snap a picture of Cameron with his helmet resting between his arm and his hip, mouthguard in hand.

---

* This rule mostly came into effect because Lisa's handwriting is super messy and I can't figure out what the word is beside Cam's name.

"You think you'll find the guy?" he asks as he puts his helmet back on.

"Hopefully," I say, backing up so I can get a wide shot with the other players out of focus in the background. A tap on my shoulder makes me jerk my camera just as I hit the shutter button. That's gonna be a blur.

I turn around to see Ben behind me, oblivious to his photography faux-pas: never surprise a photographer when the camera's up to her face.

"Whatcha doing?" he asks, putting a hand on my back. Telling him about the assignment takes about as long as it takes Cameron to return to the field.

"Are you really going to find whoever did it by taking a bunch of candids? Besides, iPods are a dime a dozen. Everyone has one."

"Not everyone. I don't have one."

"Really?" Ben can't hide his surprise. "Poor Pippa." I cringe but then he pulls me into a half hug. Most action I've seen since Reggie in the Scoops freezer. "Sounds like something Principal Forsythe should be handling. Come on, I want to shoot with you. Wouldn't you rather be taking pictures you *want* to be taking?" he teases. "Can I convince you to skip next period and shoot some threes with me?"

"My mom has a rule about skipping class. Don't."

"I have a rule about skipping class too," Ben says. "Don't get caught. And you won't, because I just told the office that you're sick and I offered to drive you home since I have a spare." His arm still around me, he turns us toward the parking lot and starts walking.

I feel all ability to resist him fading, and I give in. He asks where I parked and I explain that my mother has our only car. Instead of teasing me again, he smiles.

"Even better. So we can just take mine." He pushes a button on his keychain and the lights on a black BMW SUV at the left side of the parking lot blink twice.

"Wow, nice car," I say, feeling self-conscious.

"Yeah, it's a guilty conscience thing. My mom felt bad about making me move here for my senior year, so she bribed me." He opens the door for me, and I get in.

My phone buzzes and I jump, worried I'm getting busted, but it's Emma, texting to ask when I'm going to interview her. Word travels fast. I text her back "Tomorrow" then put my phone away. Why hasn't Dylan texted again? It's been nearly 20 hours since he asked for my number. Hasn't he had anything interesting to eat? Text me, McCuter! I push the thought out of my mind though, and try to focus on the present. I'm skipping school with Ben. Which is kind of a date. With a guy who seems pretty into me. I should be happy about that. So why am I skeptical? I don't want to judge a potential love interest by his cool clothes, car and interests, but what if my food theory also applies to boys?

"What do you think about going to the river walk?" I suggest.

The path winds alongside the Cherokee River

and stretches the whole length of Spalding. It's one of my favorite places to shoot, especially in autumn. There's a trail through the woods for walking and a paved path that runs a bit higher up, and Dad and Mom and I used to ride our bikes along there on Sundays in the summer, and then stop for a picnic in Hannover Park. And, OK, there's also this spot where people park behind the trees, right where the river turns into rapids, and it's all secluded, and they, well, you get the idea. I've never been there, at least not at night, when it counts. And even though it's super lame it's definitely on the list of things I've got to do before the end of high school. I mean, come on. Is that too much to ask?

Ben pulls out of the parking lot and makes a left onto Elm. My phone buzzes again. It's Dace calling. Before I can even say hello, she launches in. "So Cole wanted me to come watch him at football practice after school," Dace says. Cole's a senior at Spalding and the latest object of Dace's short affection span. "But I told him I don't want to sit through an entire football practice so I said I'd just meet him at Pete's Pizza after, and now he's pissed at me and told me not to bother coming at all. What the Fudgee-O?"

"Did she just say 'What the Fudgee-O?'" Ben asks.

"You can hear her?" I say to Ben. "Wait, I thought you had a go-see this afternoon?" I say to Dace.

"Who are you talking to?" Dace demands.

"You. But also Ben—"

"Ben Baxter? Pippa Greene. Where are you?"

"Skipping. I mean, I'm sick. Cover for me if necessary."

"I'm impressed. I didn't think you had it in you."

"I didn't do anything. And also, he can *hear* you," I hiss.

"Then ask him for the male perspective. What's the big deal about me watching Cole grunt and chest-bump for an hour? Is this some sort of male ego thing?"

"He doesn't care about practice," Ben says. "It's code for let's get in each other's pants under the bleachers after."

I turn to stare at him. "Are you serious?" I signal for him to turn down the gravel road shortcut.

"Positive."

"Hookup session under the bleachers," I report back to Dace.

"Figures. Wow, I can't believe I didn't think of that. *That* I'm up for. OK, I better go do damage control. Call you later."

Has Ben already made out with someone under the bleachers? He pulls into the gravel lot and parks under a row of overhanging trees, at the far end of the lot.

Ben grabs his camera out of the back, then we walk through the parking lot to the opening in the wooden fence.

"Isn't it so pretty here?" I say nervously, leading the way to the trail.

"I hadn't noticed," Ben says, and I look at him. He raises his eyebrows and I blush.

The path winds down to the water and then onto the narrow trail. I stop every so often to snap a picture. "I like the theme you chose," I say, moving slightly to get three elm trees into the upper left intersection of the nine sections of my frame.

"Can I see?" He leans close to me to check out my photo. He smells like cologne. "So you put the trees really far over there on purpose?" he asks, confused.

"Yeah. The rule of thirds," I say. He doesn't respond. "Can I see yours?" I say. Oh god, did I just say that?

"I was just messing around." He passes me his camera, but it feels like he's reluctant. I squint at the first photo. He's centered a group of four trees. Even though I really love following the rule of thirds, a lot of people break the rule and get interesting shots. But his photo lacks any sort of interesting composition. It's just a bunch of trees.

"Come here," he says, grabbing his camera back and then pulling me in for a hug. "This is fun."

I nod, aware of how close he is. There's a part of me that wishes it were Dylan here with me but I push that thought away. Dylan isn't a photographer, Ben is.

"You ready to move on?" Ben asks, and I nod, following him down the path. I ask him what his theme is for Vantage Point, but he says he's not sure. "How's your fashion theme coming along?"

"Actually, my theme is Memories." I get a bit of a sinking feeling as I tell him; I still haven't told Dace. I need to—I know that—I'm just waiting for the right time.

He gives me a funny look. "What happened to fashion?"

"I changed my mind," I say, feeling too guilty to say more.

"But you won your division last year," Ben says. "And I was reading up on the rules. You can keep the same theme two years in a row."

"I know," I say. "But I don't feel passionate about it."

Ben shakes his head. "You should stick with the sure thing. You want to win the five grand, and you know the judges liked your fashion stuff. I wouldn't mess with that. You still have the photos from last year?"

"Of course." He has a point, and I'm desperate to go to the Tisch camp—the money would be nice too—but it just doesn't feel right. I want the judge from Tisch to be impressed by my work, to remember me when I apply for college there next year.

The trail leads to the park by the waterfall. I head toward the gazebo in the middle of the grassy space. "My mom and dad got married there," I say. "Do you mind if I snap a few pics before we turn back?" It's perfect for my Memories theme—they got married in the autumn. Ben sits down on a bench near the gazebo and watches me as I move around, shooting peaks on the gazebo roof, the lines of benches, the chipped-paint stairs.

I turn back toward him and see him moving his camera away from his face. As he stands, I wonder if he was taking a picture of me, but before I can ask, he tells me that's exactly what he was doing. "You're much more interesting to look at than anything else," he says, his intense blue eyes fixed on mine as he steps toward me, stopping only when his toes are touching mine. I want to look away, but I also don't want to look away, not one bit. He moves closer even though it seems completely impossible to stand any closer to me. I feel all fluttery and weird and like everything's happening in slow motion but also at super warp speed and then before I can even register what's about to happen, his lips are on mine.

• • •

There's clearly, obviously, most definitely, something wrong with my cellphone. Why am I not getting any texts? I slap my phone against the white plastic chair I'm sitting on in Dr. Judy's waiting room.

OK. So I've gotten 17 texts from Dace. (She got to third base—literally—with Cole; that was the section of bleachers they ended up making out behind. Apparently it wasn't as sexy as it sounds, on account of all the gravel and dirt.) There are also two from Emma, one from Gemma, one from Mom and one from some random number that nearly gave me a heart attack thinking it was Dylan until I determined it was spam, probably not Dylan offering me a chance to win $1 million.

But there's only one person I want to be getting texts from, and that's Dylan. Which is crazy, because I haven't been kissed in 458 days, and the 458-day dry spell breaks, and I'm not even thinking about the guy who kissed me. Because I'm totally distracted by the guy who hasn't kissed me. Why even ask for my number if you're not going to use it, McCuter? Could he have accidentally deleted my number? Should I creep his Facebook page to see what he's up to? I'm not Facebook friends with him. And should I really friend him if he hasn't texted? Won't I look desperate? Maybe I should make a fake Facebook profile and friend him. But why would he friend someone he doesn't know and who has zero friends?

I'm totally over him.

My phone buzzes just as I'm about to turn it off and then back on again for the third time.

Dylan: Philadelphia Greene!

He texts again before I can get my fingers to stop shaking enough to text back.

Dylan: Food Alert! Ice cream sandwich. Left it on counter last night for 10 min, just so it would soften the cookie but ice cream oozed out. Looked terrible but never tasted better!

Me: U can't modify original state. It's cheating.

Dylan: Not cheating. Dedication to cause. Totally allowed. Rule #43. Didn't u get the Rule Book? Besides we're on the same team. We're in this together.

Me: Who's our competition?

Dylan: No competition. We'd blow everyone out of the water with our awesomeness.

Yeah, the part about forgetting all about Dylan? Scratch that. I'm officially back in total like with him.

· · ·

"So you kissed this boy, Ben Baxter, but you can't stop thinking about another boy," Dr. Judy says, clicking away at her laptop. I'm pretty sure she's playing Solitaire.

"Maybe it's because I've liked Dylan for so long?" I explain. "And I don't know Ben as well. So I should give Ben a chance, right? Because long term he's probably better for me."

"Let's back things up a minute. Do you think you should be kissing boys who you're not sure you like?"

"I didn't say I wasn't sure I liked Ben. I do. I just think I might like Dylan better. What I'm asking is whether it's stupid to like Dylan. And I can't really know if I like Ben if I don't give him a chance. And that means kissing."

"But you know you like Dylan and you haven't kissed him."

"Kissing doesn't really matter. Dace says kissing is basically like coughing. Not a big deal. And doesn't really tell you anything anyway."

"Is that what you think?"

Dr. Judy's specialty is asking me what I think. Which is *so* typical shrink. Correction: psychologist. But why do I have to have all the answers? If I had all the answers, would I be here?

"I don't know. I don't think I've kissed enough

to know if it makes a difference or not. Can we talk about something else?"

"No. I find this fascinating," she says, taking a sip of water. "Tell me again why you kissed Ben?"

"I didn't. He kissed me," I say again.

She pushes her glasses onto her forehead. "Did you tell him you aren't sure if you're into him?"

"When was I supposed to do that? After he kissed me? That would be kind of awkward, don't you think?"

"What do you think?"

Here we go again.

"You know what? Fine. I won't kiss him again until I'm sure. OK?" I fiddle with the hem of my shirt.

"If that's what you want. Now what about Dylan?"

"I like him. A lot. But I feel like I don't know what's going on with him. Like if he dropped out of school or what he's doing with his life. But despite that I still feel this connection to him. Is that weird?"

Dr. Judy shakes her head and, surprise, surprise, asks me if I think it's weird.

I tell her I'm not sure, and she says that it's OK to not be sure of my feelings. That that's what we're here to talk about. Then she asks me what makes me feel like I have a connection to him, and I tell her I'm not sure about that either, that it's just a gut feeling. That I feel safe around him.

"Listen," Dr. Judy says, "why don't we make a pact just to see how things play out this week. You call or text or see whoever you feel like, without worrying about what they'll think or want from you. If you want to call the same boy three days in a row, do it. And then if you want to see the other boy, do that. And we'll meet next week and you'll tell me all about it." Dr. Judy uncrosses her legs and then crosses them the other way. "Now how are things going in the hospital? How is it making you feel about your father?"

I make something up, about how the hospital seems to be helping, and the session ends a few minutes later. My circular reasoning continues on the bus ride home. Maybe the only reason I like Dylan is historical? And Ben likes me, and we have tons in common. And he's driven. Or at least not a college dropout, or whatever. And just because I had thought of him as my competition doesn't mean I have to keep thinking of him like that. Maybe he could be my boyfriend. Maybe I need to shift my focus from Dylan the slacker to Ben.

• • •

Dylan: Food Alert! Just had a Wardinski's hot dog. Oldest hot dog in Western New York. Fully loaded.

Me: Oldest hot dog? That doesn't sound very good.

Dylan: It might kill me. But it was totally worth it.

Flirting about old hot dogs. Well, there's a first time for everything.

"So I have the perfect solution," Dace says. She's on my bed, pretending to do homework but is really on Instagram. I'm going through my Vantage Point photos.

"We have a problem?" I ask, distracted as I scroll through the photos in my Vantage Point folder. I've been putting contenders in the folder over the past few months, ever since I thought of the Memories theme. I can only show my best six, but right now there are almost two dozen pics. I flag a picture of the gazebo in Hannover Park, the yellowed album page from the garage sale, and the doors to the Train Station—where Dad and I saw the David Westerly exhibit.

"Yes. And the solution is a pool party."

"A pool party? Isn't it a little late in the season?"

"It's going to be 70 degrees this weekend. We

have to take advantage of it. That's why I'm calling it the Indian Summer Pool Party. Saturday. Vivs and Fred are going to some medical convention in Vegas. You know what that means: what happens when the parents are in Vegas . . ."

"Doesn't get back to them in Vegas?"

"Exactly. Ooh, that's the perfect name for the party. WHWTPAIV."

"Really rolls off the tongue."

"And you're inviting Funeral Boy. And Ben."

"Um, no. I'm too stressed about Vantage Point. I don't have time for a party. Besides, I don't ask guys out. I want Dylan to ask *me* out."

"Wow. I didn't realize it was 1952."

"I'm sure he doesn't want to come to a high school party anyway . . ."

"Excuse me, it's not a high school party. I'm inviting Asher, and he's not in high school." Asher is this guy who works at a bar and, in theory, goes to community college.

"What about Cole?"

"I'm inviting him too."

"You can't invite both of them."

"Of course I can. It's a party. The point's to invite lots of people. So you should do the same." She hops off the bed. "I'm going to get something to drink. Want anything?"

I shake my head. A picture of Dylan spans my computer screen. Dr. Judy said to have fun. Maybe I should be more like Dace and just have a few boys on the go at the same time—at least for a week.

When Dace returns, I tell her she's right—maybe

I'll try to date both guys. But she just laughs. "Oh no," she says, shaking her head. "You're a one-guy kind of girl. You have to choose. That's why you invite both guys—nothing like a little healthy competition to see who steps up their game to win your eternal affection. It's the natural selection process. Like in the wild when the ape eats the antelope."

"I don't think apes eat antelopes. Ants maybe, but not antelopes," I say.

"You get the idea," Dace says. "A Natural Selection Party. NSP for short."

How many names is this party going to have?

"Can you take Mr. Winters to his chemo treatment?" Hannah asks, looking up from her chart. "Room 318. They're understaffed on the third floor."

I register this information, then shake my head.

"No?" She looks at me incredulously.

"I'll do it." Ashley—one of the other volunteers— is standing behind me. "You're crazy," she whispers. "It's the *best* job. You just take them there and hang out with the other candystripers, and it practically takes up the whole shift." She smirks at me, grabs the form from Hannah, and practically skips down the hall to the elevator. Suddenly it makes sense why there's never anyone around when someone soils their sheets, and I'm the sucker who cleans up the mess.

Hannah tells me to mop up a spill in front of room 422. There's an orderly in the supply closet, returning a mop and pail. Why am I cleaning up a spill if that's a job a paid employee does? More importantly, will I ever be in the supply closet to make out rather than to get a mop? Right now, it seems as unlikely as not having any more panic attacks.

Thankfully, after cleaning the spill, Hannah rewards me with flowers. Not like, she gives me flowers. But she says I can deliver them. Apparently the Handy Helpers—volunteers over 60—usually deliver the flowers but someone called in sick. The florist is in the atrium, which is obviously my favorite spot in the entire hospital (until the supply closet takes over as makeout central) because of the Dylan sighting, but today he's not there. The florist disappears into the walk-in fridge and returns with a large bouquet of blue and pink flowers and two balloons— one that says "It's a Girl!" and the other that says "It's a Boy!" Shouldn't you be sure of the sex before sending flowers? Then I realize, duh, it must be twins. Maybe this whole place isn't all about death, dying, disease and the land of eternal depression after all.

"Flower delivery," I say, knocking on room 242, the way the woman at the florist instructed me. There's a quiet "Come in" so I push open the door and walk in. A woman about my mom's age lies on the bed. She gives a half-hearted smile when she sees me. "These are for you, I think," I say, looking at the tag. "Shelby?"

She nods. "Thanks. You can put them over there." She points to the window, where there's a mountain of bouquets and baskets piled on the sill and below. There has to be at least a dozen bouquets of flowers, two dozen balloons and an army of teddy bears of all different sizes and colors.

I set the bouquet down. "Wow, you're popular," I say. But she doesn't look very happy. Dark moons underline her eyes, and I realize, this woman hasn't had a good night's sleep for weeks.

"My twins were born three months early."

"Oh, are they OK?"

She says that they're in the NICU, the neonatal intensive care unit, because they only weigh two pounds each. "I hate that they have to be there. I'm there so much the nurses kicked me out, actually. They said I need to get my rest." She sighs. "They're beautiful."

"Congratulations?" I say. "Er—I'm sorry?"

She almost laughs. "I know—I'm confused too. I don't know whether to be happy I have two beautiful babies or scared for them because they were born prematurely. So it's almost like I'm not letting myself feel anything."

"You have to let yourself feel your feelings," I say. "That's what I hear, anyway."

"Thank you," she says. "Feel my feelings—I'm going to think about that."

Four floors, nine bouquets and an hour later, I'm going up on the elevator on the way to the fourth floor, having one of those think-sessions that tend to happen on otherwise empty elevators. There's so much pain in this building, it's hard not to let it all get you down. There was a little boy lying still in his bed, an old man with a broken hip, another mom with some weird leg infection and another couple of people who didn't have any idea yet what was wrong with them. The only thing they knew is that they felt like crap. Those hurt the most. I'd seen the beginnings of that story before, and I knew how it ended.

Then the doors open on 3, and Dylan walks onto my elevator.

"Hey," I say, mustering a smile.

He looks up at me, somewhere else, and for a moment I have this weird feeling he's totally forgotten who I am. "Oh hey," he says. No smile. Nothing. Actually he looks miserable. He presses the button for the ground floor even though the elevator is going up. "Oh," he says. He looks at me. To see whether I noticed? And the whites of his eyes are kind of gray and his skin looks ashen. Dark circles. He looks down at the book in his hand.

"What are you reading?" I ask him.

"Oh, uh . . . what?" he says, distracted.

"Hey, are you OK?"

"Yeah, yeah, just um . . . sorry, I'm just a bit preoccupied."

"Oh."

Don't get distracted . . .

"So actually," I say, "it's great that I ran into you. I wanted to invite you . . ."

The doors open on the fourth floor.

He manages a weak smile.

"Your floor," he says.

"Of course," I say. My floor. There's some magnetic force keeping me on the elevator but I push against it and step out. The doors are closing just as I turn around. He's looking down at his book again.

What just happened?

My phone buzzes and for a split second I think
it's him.

Dace: U ask Funeral Boy to party?

Ugh. It's like she's psychic. I start to type out
what just happened, then delete it.

Me: No.

Dace: Well what r u waiting for? U don't want
ur new bikini to go to waste do u?

Me: What new bikini?

Dace: The one Abercrombie says he can't
wait to c u in. He's coming. 1 down 1 to go!

• • •

"He totally brushed me off. I was there, I was about
to ask him to the party and instead he told me, basically, to get off the elevator. There wasn't anything
friendly about it. It was like he didn't want me to be
there. Not like I was a friend, like I was someone he
didn't like. He *despised*. You should have seen it—it
was his whole manner. "

I'm laying on my right side on the bed, looking at
17-year-old Dad on the wall.

"Ugh, I thought things were *good*. Oh, and Ben's
coming to the party. Dace says *because* of me.

Which is cool. But I just wish Dylan were coming. Even though he totally brushed me off. Ugh—why do I *care* so much?"

I roll onto my back and stare at the ceiling. Maybe his brush-off had nothing to do with me? Maybe he had other things on his mind. Maybe he has a thing about personal conversations on elevators? What if I hadn't seen him on the elevator—then what? Am I seriously going to throw away a chance at love with Dylan, all because Ben jumped my lips quicker and the elevator doors opened before I could ask Dylan to the party? I sit up and grab my phone off my nightstand and bring up Dylan on the text message screen.

Me: Chip n dip Alert! Tmw @ Dace's. Pool party included. Wanna come?

And then I watch the screen, waiting for his response to come. Which is how I must have fallen asleep, because a couple of hours later I wake up with the phone still in my hand. The clock says 3:19 a.m. "Yep," I say to my dad. "It's that pitiful." I put the phone on my nightstand and turn off my light.

Why *hasn't* Dylan replied to my text? Isn't it common courtesy to reply? How hard is it to just type "Yes" or "No"? It's not hard at all. It's a few buttons plus the Enter button. It's EASY.

And then, while packing my stuff for Dace's, I get a text.

Dylan: Yes! What time?

He said yes. He didn't delete me from his phone. He likes me. Or doesn't *not* like me. My fingers are shaking as I text back, giving him Dace's address and telling him to come anytime after 4.

● ● ●

Dace was a bit concerned about her parents finding out about the party if I told Mom.

THE RISKS IN TELLING MOM ABOUT THE PARTY

She could tell Dace's parents.
She could forbid me to go.
She could forbid me to go and tell Dace's parents.

THE RISKS IN NOT TELLING MOM ABOUT THE PARTY

She could find out.
I could be grounded for life for lying.

That would be the end of Sleepover Saturdays.

The deciding factor came down to the fact that this Saturday we were supposed to be sleeping at my house. If we changed it, my mom would be suspicious. So I told my mom. Which went over surprisingly well, though she did have a few rules, which she typed up at work (shouldn't she be busier with sick animals?) and handed to me when she got home from the clinic:

MOM'S PARTY RULES

1. No drugs
2. No drinking
3. No sleepover

"Are we clear?" Mom asks.

"Yeah, I'll put this through the laminator so it doesn't get wet at the party. That way I can keep referring to it all night."

"Pippa . . ." Mom says warningly.

"I'm kidding! I got it." I'm not worried about the drugs part—at least, me doing them. Dace and I tried smoking pot last summer but it made me lethargic and boring, and I'm not about to start doing something more hardcore. Besides, I like drinking just fine. So #2 is definitely going to be a problem since the definition of a party when you're in high school is "excuse to drink while someone's parents are away."

But #3? "No sleepover?"

"NO sleepover," Mom says.

"But we can't break tradition."

"No sleepover or no party."

"But if I don't sleep over I won't be able to help Dace clean up. Not that we plan on making a mess, but we can't control what everyone does. Not that there will be a lot of people, but there will be boys. Not a lot of boys . . ."

I was digging myself my own pool.

"*If* everyone is still at the party when you leave, which I would suggest is not a good idea anyway, but if they are, then you can go back in the morning to help Dace clean up. Home by eleven."

"One."

"Midnight. And not a second later."

● ● ●

My mom may have had some rules, but Dace and I have a few rules of our own.

DACE & PIPPA'S PARTY RULES
1. No one gets in the house.
2. If you're about to let someone in the house, remember Rule #1.

"*We're* still using the bathroom in the house, though, right?" I ask as we walk out to the backyard. Dace is carrying a pitcher of lemonade and two glasses on a tray and I've got a stack of trashy magazines. Our towels are wrapped around our waists. "The last thing I want to do is pee in the poolhouse after 50 other drunk people have gone in there."

Dace nods and removes her towel, revealing her orange bikini bottom.

"You mixed?" I say, eyeing her pink top as she removes the strap around her neck.

"I couldn't settle on just one. I guess I like my bikinis like I like my boys. Two at a time," she says, laying her towel on her lounge chair. I do the same and sit down.

"Only two? I thought you liked to have at least three on the go at once," I joke, adjusting the top of the blue-and-white striped bikini that Dace lent me—she got a whole bunch of cute bikinis from one of her shoots. It's a perk, for sure, but I still feel self-conscious. I don't exactly fill it out in the right places the way Dace does.

"Good point." She rattles off the list of invited

guys who are definitely potential makeout partners: "Kevin, Cole, Asher . . ."

"Aren't you worried each of them will think you've already got a boyfriend and back off?"

Dace takes a sip of her lemonade. "Worried? No. Boys love a little healthy competition. They're like soda. Some are like Pepsi, always trying to be better than Coke. The Cokes know they're the best, but are always on their A-game because the Pepsis are hanging around."

"What about if they're root beer?"

"Root beers are the wild card. A little crazy."

I stand up and walk over to the edge of the pool. The pool is L-shaped—the main part is just like a normal swimming pool, except with a gradual beach entry on one side, so you wade in from the deck. Then in the deep end, the other part has this little diving area and there are not one, but two diving boards. And then there's a hot tub and a sauna. Total resort.

I hit the higher diving board. "Request?"

"Double twist-triple-toe-loop-back-flip!" she yells from her lounger. Right.

I swan dive into the water. It's pretty much my only dive. In the summer I almost had a flip down pat, but I haven't practiced in a while and if I land on my back it hurts like a mother. And makes my back totally red. Not attractive.

After a few more dives I do some laps, then climb out and walk over to the lounge chair beside Dace's. I shake my hair out over her, letting the beads of water spray her. She squeals.

I lay down on the lounger. Dace tops up her glass with lemonade and pours me a glass. I take a sip.

"Um. Not lemonade."

"Yes, but spiked. The best kind. I can't believe Fred thought hiding the key to the liquor cabinet in his sock drawer was a good idea." She takes a sip. "So good, right?"

"Yum." And so wrong. Oh so wrong. "I can't get wasted, remember. I have to be home by midnight. Mom's rules." The rules I threw in Dace's bedroom trash bin. "And I have to work on my Vantage Point entry tomorrow."

"Come on. It's 3:30. You'll be sober by the time you go home. Also, this is just a little something to loosen you up," she says, taking her bikini top off.

"Dace!" The backyard is big—but it isn't *that* big. The neighbors can totally see over the fence—especially from the second story.

"What? I don't want tan lines," she says.

"Tan lines? How is that even possible? You've religiously worn sunscreen since, like, the fifth grade."

She shakes her head. "Not today. I'm breaking all my sunscreen rules. Guess it's a rules-breaking kind of day."

"What will Elise say if you get a burn?"

"With any luck, that I can't do the Cheektowaga car show."

"Why don't you just tell her you don't want to do it?"

"I tried. But she said it's that or back to mall fashion shows. This is all Viv's fault. If she'd have let me go to Japan when I signed with Elise, then I wouldn't even be talking about some dumb Cheektowaga *car show*." She sighs. "I'm sorry. Are you freaking out?"

I look at her, confused. "What do you mean?"

"Just—the pact. For our future. You must be a bit worried how we're going to make it happen when I'm dicking around. I'm just in a rut. I'm sorry."

My stomach drops. The guilt almost makes me tell Dace about my Vantage Point theme. That I've moved on from fashion to memories. If it were anyone else, it might be worth it so that she felt like I'm not adding any additional pressure for her to make it big, but I know better. With Dace, she'll just think I'm bailing on her. Even though it has nothing to do with her at all.

"You'll get to Japan," I say. "And in the meantime, I like having you here. I'd miss you if you took off." Going to Japan is important if you want to make it— apparently you go there for a year, do a billion shoots and after that you can pretty much get any editorial job. But I really can't imagine being at Spalding without Dace. That's the hard thing about friendship, you want what's best for your best friend, but sometimes it's not what's best for yourself.

"Thanks. Let's just get drunk and forget all about this, K?"

"OK. You should probably put your top back on before everyone gets here. You're going to give your mantourage the wrong idea."

"Maybe that's the right idea," Dace says with a coy smile, but obliges.

Dace is still a virgin, even though she totally

doesn't act like it. Some of our other friends are having sex, but we both want to wait. Dace, despite being a super-flirt, doesn't want to have sex with a guy if she doesn't want to be his girlfriend, and right now, she doesn't want to be anyone's girlfriend. Dace has been talking more and more about doing it though, just to get it over with so it's not such a big deal. I'm worried about that because it *is* a big deal, but also because, if she starts having sex and I'm not, I feel like we won't be as close anymore. It's silly, because we're best friends and one little thing like that shouldn't matter but I still worry it will.

"Hey girls!" Emma and Gemma call as they come through the gate to the backyard. Carrying overnight bags. *Overnight?* They're staying over? I stifle the surge of jealousy.

"Any word on your iPod?" I ask Emma as I follow her inside so they can drop off their things. The story comes out on Friday, but so far there haven't been any leads on the thief. She shakes her head and says her mom's mad at her for being so irresponsible for losing it, but Gemma believes her that someone outright stole it.

An hour later the backyard's packed, and so's the pool. Dace's iPod is connected to the sound system—the playlist she made at the start of summer on repeat for one final hurrah. I'm contemplating another glass of spiked lemonade when I feel an arm slip around my waist. I turn to face Ben, who pulls me in for a soft kiss. When we break, I kind of want to wipe off my lips—he's a really *wet* kisser.

"Hey babe," he purrs.

Babe?

"Nice bikini," he says, totally talking to my chest.

"Do you want a drink?" I ask, noticing he's empty handed aside from his leather satchel, slung across his body. It's a known fact that parties are BYOB—but maybe they did things differently wherever Ben used to go to school.

"Sure—a beer'd be great."

Dace is at the cooler with a guy, who, when he stands up, looks like he could be Ben's Abercrombie twin: polo shirts, khakis and deck shoes.

"Cole, this is Pippa!" Dace says happily, and I give a small wave. Ben puts his arm around me protectively and kisses me on the ear, then throws his hand up in a sort of hey-wave. "Ben," he says to Cole.

"Beer?" Cole asks Ben, holding out a can. Ben takes it.

"So you go to Spalding with the girls?" Cole asks as I untangle myself from Ben. Dace pours another spiked lemonade from the jug on the table and hands it to me, takes a sip of her own, then links arms with me and leads me away from them. "Oh swoon," she whispers. "Isn't that cute? Our boys are getting along."

"He's not my boy," I say defensively. I don't want to be with Ben by default. Where is Dylan?

"Would you relax and have fun? Ben's crazy about you. What's the problem?"

"Sorry," I say, but I'm not feeling it. If Ben's going to be my boyfriend, shouldn't I be thinking about him?

"Ooh, there's Asher," Dace says, clinking glasses with me and sauntering over to the gate. I pull on my cover-up, then find Emma and hang out with her and a bunch of other girls in our class for a while, until Ben is back at my side.

"What do you say we get out of here for a bit? I need some Pippa time," he says, wrapping his arm around my waist and pulling me close.

"Well, I don't want to be a bad party host," I say. Where *is* Dylan?

"It's not your party, it's Dace's. And you'd be a good host to me."

Ben grabs my hand and starts leading me around the side of the house.

"Hang on, I just have to pee," I say once we get through the gate to the side of the house. He follows me up the steps, wrapping his arms around my waist from behind as I grab the key and unlock the door, then put the key back under the mat. "Pretend you didn't just see that. And you have to wait here," I say, one hand on the doorknob.

"Why?"

"Nobody's allowed in the house. If you have to go to the bathroom, you have to use the poolhouse. I'm sorry, but Dace'll kill me if I break the rules."

"Come on. You can trust me," he begs, his big blue eyes wide and sad, like a puppy dog.

I shake my head. He comes closer and nuzzles on my ear, which tickles, even though I bet it's supposed to feel sexy. I squirm away but I can't back up since I'm already pressed against the door. I *really* have to pee.

"I'll just be a second."

"And I'll just wait inside the door. Surely it's not breaking the rule if I'm not *doing* anything inside the house."

"Um . . ." Does his logic make sense? Between the spiked lemonades and my bladder, I can't focus. I turn the door handle and . . . he's inside. "Wait here," I say, pointing at the floor like he's a dog. But he doesn't listen. Instead of using the bathroom on the main floor, I race up the stairs, thinking I can get away from him and he'll stay downstairs, but that's obviously faulty logic, because he follows me right up the stairs. As I pass Vivian's room, I see Cole by the bed with Dace. Whoops. I guess she's breaking our only rule too.

Dace's room is two doors down. "You wait here for me." I say, pushing him inside. I shut the door, thinking he's at least hidden if Dace comes out, though really, if she finds him in there she'll probably be more upset with me for letting him in her room at all. I'll just blame it on the spiked lemonade. And besides, I highly doubt she's coming out of her mom's room anytime soon.

"I missed you," Ben says as soon as I return to Dace's room.

"I was only gone a minute."

He shuts the door behind me, pressing me up against it. "It was too long. Too long to be away from a girl I like so much."

"You're so direct."

"Isn't it good to be direct? To be honest?"

I sneak a peek at the clock on the dresser.

It's nearly 11. If Dylan wasn't going to come, he should've said so.

Ben grabs my waist and turns me around so we're facing the mirror on the back of the door. "We look good together," he says. "Don't you think?" But it's clear he's looking at himself. My reflected image goes red as he nuzzles my ear.

"I'm going to kiss you now."

And before I can say anything, he's spinning me back around and then his lips are on mine. Again. And I can't help thinking what Dr. Judy would say.

"We should go back outside," I say, taking a step back. He smells like beer.

"Or we could stay here," Ben says.

He pulls me closer. "Come on . . ." he says, trying to lead me over to the bed. To second base. Oh no. I am staying firmly on first base. No more bases are going to be passed today. "I thought you were into me," he says. It's almost a whine.

"I am," I say. Face it, Pippa. Dylan's not coming. I try to think clearly: I'm in Dace's room with a boy who's totally into me. Who tells me he likes me. Who wants to kiss me. And I like him. Right? And Dr. Judy told me to do what I want this week, without worrying about the outcome.

I'm just not actually sure I can do that. Or if I want to.

"I'm not sure if I like you in that way," I say, then instantly regret it. "I mean, yet."

He looks annoyed, then his face softens. "You're not sure, huh?"

"It's just . . . It's all happening a bit fast. Maybe if

we just talked a bit. Tell me more about you. Or . . . Buffalo. Or what your favorite TV show is."

"I think if I kiss you some more, you'll know a lot quicker if you like me or not than if I tell you about my favorite TV show."

He leans into me and we're kissing, just like that. I try to concentrate on the kissing itself, and channeling his tongue inside my mouth rather than all over it. He kisses like Emma's golden retriever. No, it's fine. There's nothing wrong with soft and slobbery kisses. They're romantic, not rough. That's nice! Of course it is. But how does Dylan kiss? I bet there's the perfect amount of roughness, just like his hands.

Stop thinking about Dylan while kissing Ben!

"Maybe we should go back outside," I say, peeling myself away.

"That bed looks pretty good. We could just lie here and talk," he says.

"Nice try . . ." I open the door.

He sighs, but grabs his satchel and follows me out of Dace's room and back down the stairs.

"Walk me out?" he says when we get to the bottom.

"You're going?" I'm not really surprised. He mumbles something about a curfew.

"Oh," I say, nodding. "Of course, you should go then." He tells me he'll text me later, but he doesn't call me babe and he doesn't kiss me again, not even on the cheek.

There's no use in me staying any longer either. Dylan's obviously not coming. I don't know why

I even let myself think for a minute he'd actually show up. Back upstairs in Dace's room I take off my cover-up and pull my white T-shirt and stretchy skirt overtop of my bikini, throw my Tisch hoodie on, then pull my hair into a messy topknot. My flip-flops are at the back door. Dace is out by the pool, standing at the end of a lounge chair. Asher is either trying to undo her bathing suit ties or hang on to them to stay somewhat vertical-ish. Either way, he isn't succeeding. She swats him away and then throws her arms around me. "Don't gooooooo."

"Be good," I say.

I walk around to the side gate and pull it open. Dylan is standing on the other side. My breath catches in my throat.

"Philadelphia Greene," he says.

But there's movement behind him: Callie.

Callie?

"Are we too late?" she says.

Callie's wearing a tiny white sundress, blue and white wedges and her hair is in a side-braid. She looks really good.

"Kind of," I say, not completely able to hide my disappointment. "I've got to be home soon. But go on in—there's still a bunch of people there."

I go to brush past him, but Dylan grabs my arm. "Hey, wait a sec?" Dylan asks, then turns to Callie. "Thanks for the ride. You stay. I'll just walk home."

"You sure?" Callie asks, and Dylan nods.

"OK. I'm gonna go in for a bit," she says. She kisses Dylan on the cheek, gives me a smile and then pushes open the gate to the backyard.

I start walking to the front of the house, and Dylan follows alongside me.

"Sorry I'm so late," he says. "How was the party?"

"Fun, I guess," I say.

Dace is able to play it cool better than me. She could be the angriest person alive but you wouldn't know it unless she wanted you to. In the last three months I've probably talked about my feelings more than I ever had in the previous 16 years, and they still remain a mystery to me. I don't have any control over them. When I know I should be full of emotion, and letting it show, I can't even muster up a tear, but then when I'd rather just be cool and fun, all I can do is over-obsess.

"Hey, what's wrong?" Dylan asks.

"Nothing!" I say, and I force a smile. "You know, you didn't have to come if you already had plans tonight with Callie."

"Plans, yes, I guess—I . . . I was playing a show."

He invited Callie to a show I didn't know he had?

"How was it?" I steal a look at him to see him running a hand through his hair.

"I'm really messing this up, aren't I?" He shoves his hands in his pockets and shrugs. "I didn't invite you because I figured you were busy with the party. And Callie was already coming to see me play . . ."

"Oh," I say.

"Anyway, I'm glad you invited me," he says.

"You are?"

We just look at each other.

"I have an idea," he says. "How much time do you have? What's your curfew?"

My watch gives me less than half an hour until I have to be home. "Midnight."

"We can do it," Dylan says. "But we have to run." He starts down the driveway.

"You're serious?" His goofy half-run is kind of hilarious. I start jogging behind him. He tells me it's worth it and I speed up.

"Flip-flops. Not. Really. Appropriate. Footwear," I say, panting. He laughs and grabs my hand as we run down the middle of the deserted street. A minute later he slows to a walk, leading me from the lit road down a darkened dirt path between two houses.

We're headed toward the ravine, but using an entrance I've never taken. It takes a minute for my eyes to adjust to the darkness. As though sensing my apprehension, Dylan squeezes my hand tighter. But it's not the walk that's making me nervous. The path narrows through the trees so that we have to go single file. "You have to duck a bit," he says, dropping my hand, and I do, the bottom branches just brushing the top of my head as I follow him down a hill. Eventually the path comes out at a wooden bridge over a creek I never knew existed. I put my hands on the railing and Dylan comes up and stands behind me, placing his arms on the railing beside mine, so that he's sort of hugging me from behind, without actually wrapping his arms around me.

"Wait a second, then you'll see."

As though someone flipped a switch, the sky lights up with tiny stars. Only they're not stars.

I gasp, wishing I had my camera. "It's beautiful. What is it?"

"Fireflies," Dylan says, his breath warm on my neck. It sends chills up and down, in the best possible way.

"But aren't they usually out in the summer?"

"It's because it's so warm. They'll only live a few days. The energy to light up zaps all their life from them. Sad but beautiful." Neither of us says anything for a few moments, the only sound the hum of the fireflies' vibration in the night air.

"I should get you home," he says, his breath warm. "Even though I could stand here all night with you. I really like you, Philadelphia Greene."

"I like you too," I whisper, not wanting to break the spell.

He puts his hands on my waist and turns me around so I'm facing him. Oh, his eyes, the stubble, his dimple . . . On my face I can feel the warmth of his breath. Wrigley's Spearmint? He brushes a strand of hair away from my face and those beautiful green eyes are getting closer, closer, closer . . .

"WHO LET THE DOGS OUT?" blasts my phone.

Oh my god, seriously?

No, really, *seriously?*

Dylan kind of shakes himself. Our eyes meet. Yes, his gaze says, the worst-timed phone call in the history of the world was *not* a figment of my imagination.

"WHO? WHO? WHO?" asks my phone, as I walk up the hill to answer it. It's like my phone is taunting me, asking me if I know. I haven't even kissed Dylan, but I know the answer to which boy. It couldn't be any clearer.

It takes us forever—or at least the entirety of *Breakfast Club*—to clean up. Dace makes a rule that we can't talk about the guys until we're done. Which is pure torture but mostly I think she just doesn't want to talk, period, because she's so hungover. A million years later, we put the last garbage bag in the garage, and then set ourselves up with another round of Advil, coffees and bacon and sit on the stools at the breakfast bar.

"OK now, where to start?" Dace says, and I give her a look. "Yeah, you win. Funeral Boy first." All Dace knows is that Dylan showed up at the party with Callie but didn't come in. I recap the 34 glorious minutes we were together.

"But no kiss?" Dace says.

"No, no kiss. And then I ran home and that was it. But it was super romantic. Seriously though, in hindsight, why was I so adamant about making curfew?"

"No clue. But you're cute," Dace says. "So . . . Funeral Boy, then?"

"Hands down. It was perfection." I sigh. "OK, tell me what happened with you. I witnessed rounds 1 and 2, but am I missing any others?"

"Rounds 1 and 2 of what?"

"Cole and Asher."

"I didn't hook up with Cole." She makes a face. "Actually I barely saw him the whole night. Why— did you see him?"

I tell her how I saw her—at least I thought I did— with Cole in her mom's room. It was definitely Cole.

"You were breaking the rule?" she asks, picking at a slice of bacon.

"Sorry."

"So he was in Viv's room with a girl?"

I nod. Dace's face clouds over, and she takes another swig of coffee. I feel bad about swooning over Dylan; she probably didn't have the best night with either guy. But she stands up again and shakes it off.

"Oh well, whatever," she says, picking up her phone and studying it. "Asher and I did it last night," she says, as though it's every day that you have sex for the first time. My mouth literally drops open. Dace taps something into her phone, then puts it back—face down—on the table. I don't know if it's the fact that I know she's not a virgin now and I still am, but somehow, despite being totally hungover, with ashen skin and matted hair, she looks even more glam than ever.

"And I thought my non-kissing moment was epic."

"Don't sweat it, Pip. It'll happen for you too, eventually."

"So . . . is Asher gonna get to be your boyfriend now?"

Dace rolls her eyes at me and goes around the breakfast bar to the main counter. "Sex does not equal lifelong commitment. It was no big deal." She pours herself more coffee from the carafe.

"Really?"

"Well, I don't want to spoil it for you," she says, moving to fill up my cup but stopping when she realizes I haven't touched it. "Anyway, it's indescribable. You'll need to find out for yourself." She puts the carafe back on the warmer.

Fears officially realized: it does change things. This is why I didn't want one of us to have sex before the other. She's acting differently already. Like I can't handle it. Maybe I can't.

Dylan: Food Alert! Cherry Blasters playing
free outdoor concert tomorrow night at
Hanlan's Field. They're kinda scruffy hipster.
Want to go and test the theory — do ugly
guys with food name make good music?

Mom is not thrilled with the idea of me going to a concert on a school night. And she is even less thrilled with the idea of me going to a concert with a guy she's never heard of. "Mom, don't worry about it, he's a nice guy, he got accepted to Harvard!" is my comeback to that one.

"It's October, Pippa," she says, and already I can see this comeback has backfired. "If he was accepted at Harvard, why isn't he *at* Harvard?"

"Mom, just trust me, OK?"

She makes a couple more protests—she doesn't like the sound of this, please be careful, she doesn't want me making a habit of going out on school nights, don't I have homework to do, blah blah blah. And then: permission granted. I don't even care that I have to be home by 11. The concert starts at eight and there's only one opener and Cherry Blasters only have two albums so, yeah, 11. Probably it'll be over a bit after 10, actually, but I want a bumper in there so that I have some time before I get that blast of "Who Let the Dogs Out?" With a few more Dylan-ward texts the plan's established: we're meeting at 6, after my shift at St. Christopher's.

Highlights of the day before the night of: lunch is a photo club meeting that sees us going around sharing our Threes photos. I almost think Ben's not going to show up, but he eventually does, about fifteen minutes into the meeting. He sits at the end of the table, not making eye contact with any of us. When it's his turn, he flicks through an iPad photo album, and it's weird. I recognize a couple of the photos from our afternoon in the park—three trees, three logs, three flagpoles I somehow missed. But once again his photos are not quite right. The angles are all off. They lack any sense of composition. They're nothing like the pictures he showed us last week. Maybe he's just having an off week?

I go last, after Gemma. Then there's a moment where you can feel the room's tension. "About next week's theme," I say, and everybody flicks to everyone else's gaze. "Any ideas?"

Nada. Zilch. Zip. Which is what I was kind of hoping. "So," I say, "what if we just skip the theme this week?"

"Yeah," Jeffrey agrees. "I'm pretty busy putting my entry together for Vantage Point."

As are we all, Jeffrey. As. Are. We. All.

After school is fun with sick people. I'm back on flower delivery. I guess because I did such a good job last week? Every time I take an elevator I expect Dylan to get on. But no, it's all uneventful until I pick up a skateboard-shaped cookie, decorated with every type of candy imaginable. The address tag lists a room on the fourth floor, back in the Rehabilitation Ward.

"Howie?" I say as I knock on the door, guessing the patient's name based on the icing inscription on the candy skateboard. I push open the door and find a boy, about 11, lying on the bed. The cast that goes ankle to thigh has about a thousand signatures on it. His eyes widen when he sees the edible skateboard.

"Holy crap, bring that over here," he says, and I carry it over to the bed. A real skateboard rests against the wall beside the head of his bed. He notices my camera around my neck. "Hey, you take pictures?"

I say yes, and he asks if that's what I want to be when I grow up, which I think is funny to hear, but it's true. He tells me he wants to be a pro skateboarder.

"Is that how you broke your leg?" I ask and he nods. "You must be pretty bummed out."

He shrugs. "Nah. I almost landed an eight-step handrail. Now I know I can do it. Soon as I get this off. Will you take my pic? I want to remember this."

The first shots are him with the candy skateboard, and then he gets me to grab his actual skateboard. "Here's how I did it," he says, lifting the skateboard up, then maneuvering it over the railing on the side of the bed. I snap a bunch of pics of Howie in action, first focusing in on the skateboard, letting Howie go out of focus behind, then vice versa.

"I'm probably not supposed to take your picture without your mom or dad's approval," I realize aloud, then I assure him I'll send him the pics and won't do anything else with them. I help him back into bed and tell him I have to go. By the time I leave Howie's room I'm in a really good mood. Back downstairs, I grab a delivery for the third floor. It's only once I'm off the elevator—actually, it's only once I'm, like, right there at the door, about to knock—that I glance at the tag to make sure I have the right room. Room 334, the tag says. And my legs nearly give out beneath me. Room 334.

I lean up against the wall and close my eyes and try to take a deep breath but I can't get enough air. Room 334.

There's the supply closet, just down the hall from the waiting room where I'd hunch down in a chair and watch TV when everything in the room got to be too much, or when my parents had something adults-only to discuss. There's the poster: *Washing Hands Saves Lives.* Which I always wondered about—prevents a few flu cases, maybe, but saves *lives?* It seemed a little overblown to me. And there's the nurses' station I've been avoiding. It's a bit past 5 on a Tuesday afternoon—Rishna's the nurse on duty unless the schedules have changed. She had the best stories. The one she told me right near the end, about how she woke up in the middle of the night to find a strange cat in her house. Her color-blind husband had let it in. He'd thought it was their cat.

I take a long slow breath. Everything's going to be OK. Lots of patients have come and gone from this room. It's just a room. It's been cleaned. It's been sanitized. There's nothing left in that room that has any memories at all. There's just someone else in there, a little earlier on the same journey that ends with a daughter no longer having her dad around.

Or whatever.

Three more deep breaths. My eyes focus on the numerals: 334. My camera clacks against the door as I set the arrangement on the floor. Then, focus: the door number in the right third of the frame, the other two-thirds filled by the hallway I walked so many times. That's right: concentrate on the rule of thirds, so you don't concentrate on anything else.

●　●　●

Dylan's carrying a blue blanket and I'm carrying the Cherry Blaster candies he gave me when he picked me up in front of the hospital in his dad's *total* dad-mobile, a navy Cadillac, with a shiny wood dashboard and all the stations preset to easy listening. Not at all what I would've thought the lead singer of Rules for Breaking the Rules would be driving but, in its own way, *so* awesome.

He lays out the blanket at a spot about halfway between the stage and the concession stands, and we both look down at it. It's a plush blanket—with an enormous Buffalo Sabres logo on it.

"Wow," I say, blinking.

"Uh. Yeah," he says.

"I didn't realize you were a big hockey fan," I say.

"You know, you could probably see that thing from space."

He laughs. And then I giggle, and then I can't stop laughing, and neither can he. "Actually," Dylan says, "my dad's the fan. I guess I just kind of grabbed the first blanket I saw. Oh god, this is embarrassing . . . Are you even gonna sit on this?"

"I'll give it a shot," I say, still laughing.

"Hey, you want a drink?"

"You think you'll be able to find your way back?"

He grins. "I'll just look for the only girl on a Buffalo Sabres blanket."

Dylan heads off, picking his way among the blankets and the picnic baskets and as he goes I watch him, this boy, this easy boy, this boy who just made me laugh more than I've laughed in the whole of the previous year. He's even cuter in the viewfinder as I snap a few pictures, out of reflex.

When he comes back he hands me a Diet Coke. He's drinking water.

"Can I see?" he asks, nodding at my camera.

Does he know what he's asking? Does he know what's in that camera? A.k.a., my life?

As well as the pictures of him I just shot. The way he smiles suggests that he gets it.

It takes a minute for him to figure out how to get it into view mode. He ticks through the ones I just shot of him without comment, then continues through the rest of the images on the data card.

"Wow," he says after a while. "I love how you see the hospital through your lens."

"Passing the time," I say, but his words are comforting.

He gets to the room 334 photo and looks at me with a question.

"My dad's room," I say.

He studies the picture for a second. "I'm sorry."

My hands are busy pulling out blades of grass. Find blade, pull. Find blade, pull.

I twist the blade between my fingers and look at Dylan. "It's OK. Life goes on, right? I'm just trying to concentrate on other stuff. Vantage Point, this photography contest, for example. Top two go to a Tisch camp in New York next month. I'd learn so much. It's two weeks of hardcore photography. But the best part is that I'd be there—right at the school. And it would look good on my college apps. Tisch is my dream school."

"That's awesome."

"What about you?" I ask. "What happened with Harvard?"

He takes a sip of his water. Nods. Then explains that he deferred for a year. "I needed to get some things in order and decide if going to Harvard is what I really want to do."

There's now a patch of dirt where there used to be grass.

"I've got a few things on the go," he says.

Like what? I'm dying to ask, but then the stage lights come up. There's the unmistakable shag of the Cherry Blasters lead singer, and I say something about it to Dylan and he laughs.

"That would be a great name for a band," he says. "Unmistakable Shag."

Lots of questions occurred to me when Dylan first asked me to go to see Cherry Blasters. What would it be like, just the two of us? Even though I've had my massive crush forever, it's not like we've spent much time together. What if we had totally different concert styles? What if he hated standing up—and got mad if others stood up in front of him? Would he dance? How did he dance? And what would he think of the way I danced? And also: what did *I* think of the way I danced? But from the moment Cherry Blasters come out I realize I have nothing to worry about. Dylan grabs my hand and pulls me up, and it starts with him bobbing his head, and then I'm bobbing my head, and then my hips start moving and his are too, and there we are on the Buffalo Sabres blanket, in full-on dance mode, a mode we stay in through the whole of the rest of the concert.

The Cherry Blasters never do encores. It's kind of their thing. So when they announce the next song will be their last, I know it's going to be their big hit, "Even if You Don't," and I touch Dylan's arm and go on my tiptoes to shout into his ear, "I love this song so *much*," and then I realize, I just touched Dylan's arm. I just shouted into Dylan's ear. And it was completely natural.

"The line about being in love with a girl who doesn't love you back?" Dylan says once the lights have come up and he's gathering his ridiculous blanket under his arm. Then he puts his other arm around me.

Also completely natural.

"Only that's not it," I say as we follow the crowd toward the exit. "It's just that she has a secret and doesn't want to hurt him. I wonder what the secret is."

"It kinda doesn't matter, right? It's like trust, I guess. You either trust someone or you don't."

"I think it matters. If the secret is hurtful," I say. "What if she's worried if he finds out, it'll taint his view of her. And she just wants a fair shot with him?" We reach the car and Dylan opens the door for me.

"I don't know," I say once he's beside me in the car. "It's so deceitful. Like tricking the person into falling in love with them, without knowing everything up front."

"So I should tell you I only have three toes on my left foot? Makes it hard to wear flip-flops but I get to park in handicapped spots."

"Ha, ha," I say, then actually laugh.

"Hey, so what time do you have to be home?" He pulls out of the parking space and follows the line of cars out of the lot. "Awesome," he says after I say 11. "You game for a little celebratory snack? I think the Cherry Blasters were sufficiently deserving, no?"

"Yes," I say. And then I turn toward him. "I had such a good time tonight." He just looks at me and grins. I can't remember the last time I felt this way. It's not happy, exactly. It's more of an awareness of not being *un*happy. Buoyant. Light. Something. As we drive we talk and it's not until he's pulling into a parking lot that I register where we are.

Scoops.

Suddenly my mouth goes dry.

Dylan is saying something, but I don't know what. I lean over, putting my head between my knees, the seatbelt cutting into the side of my neck.

"Are you OK?" Dylan asks, his hand on my leg.

"Take me home. Take me home. Take me home," I say over and over. Am I saying it aloud? Can he hear me? Does he know where I live? What is he going to think of me?

Everything goes quiet.

WTF?

I open my eyes and stare at the ceiling. And then it all comes back. Again.

"Oh . . ." I roll over and stare up at my dad's photo. "Why couldn't I just be a normal teenager and get super wasted, make a total ass of myself and *then* feel like this?

I bury my head under my covers, shutting out the waft of coffee that means Mom is up, and I'm going to have to explain last night to her.

"Get up," Dad tells me. He's right. Staying in bed, replaying things, only makes things worse. Passing out in Dylan's car, waking up in the driveway. Dylan helping me to the door. The worried look on Mom's face when she let us in. Dylan explaining what happened. Mom taking me upstairs to bed. Putting a glass of water on the nightstand and kissing me goodnight. Telling me to get some rest, and not to worry. The guilt of knowing she would be sleeplessly worrying for both of us.

"Waffles," Mom says, pushing open my door with her foot, carrying a tray. She's in jeans, her hair pulled back in a ponytail. She places the tray on the bed and hands me a plate and a fork and knife. She pulls the chair from my desk and sits down, taking the other plate, and her cup of coffee.

"Why are you still home?" I ask, digging in.

"Pippa, I was worried. Wanna talk about it?"

"There's nothing to talk about."

"Really? Because you arrived home in the arms of a very nervous-looking boy who explained you'd passed out. I thought you'd been roofied."

"I was drinking Diet Coke from a bottle. I wasn't roofied." I say, putting my plate on the nightstand. Telling her I'd been roofied is probably better than telling her the truth.

"So what happened then?" she asks gently. She puts her plate on the desk and gets up, then climbs onto the bed beside me, leaning into the pillows.

I sigh. "I had another panic attack. A bad one."

"Oh honey . . ." Mom wraps her arms around me and pulls me into her for a hug. I bury my head in her shoulder. "What caused it?"

"Dylan took me to Scoops."

"But you love Scoops," Mom says, confused. I shake my head.

"I haven't been there since Dad . . ."

She squeezes me harder, and says she had no idea. "I thought you didn't have the panic attacks anymore. You told me you and Dr. Judy worked through them. Even Dr. Judy told me months ago that you weren't having them anymore."

I sniffle. "That's because I told her they'd stopped."

"But why would you lie about this?"

"Well, they had stopped, kind of. I have all these coping mechanisms Dr. Judy taught me. And it's better, it really is. It's just . . . I've been thinking about Dad a lot. And my Vantage Point theme brings back more memories of him. And I started freaking out and I didn't want to tell Dr. Judy because she was being so positive about how I wasn't having panic attacks anymore. I felt like I'd been failing her and that made me feel like I'm wasting your money by even going to see her." I haven't been this honest with my mom in months.

"Why didn't you tell me? I didn't know being at the hospital was making you feel that way." She pulls away from me so she can look me in the eye.

"I didn't want you to worry."

"Oh Pippa. I'm going to worry about you no matter what. It's my job. Like it or not. So you might as well give me concrete things to worry about," she says with a smile. "OK?"

I nod. "OK." She smoothes my hair, like she's been doing since I was little. I tuck my head back onto her shoulder.

"So this guy you went to the concert with . . ."

"Is so awesome," I moan. "And now he probably thinks I'm a total freak."

"I highly doubt that. He seemed very nice. And he

said to tell you that he was sorry for rifling through your bag, but he was trying to find something with your address on it because he didn't know where we live."

All I can think is that I'm glad I didn't have any underwear in my bag, which is such a bizarre thought because I can't even imagine why I *would* have underwear in my bag. Ever.

"This boy seemed genuinely concerned about you," Mom says, retrieving her coffee and taking a sip. She sits back on the desk chair.

I pull my legs under me.

"Can you really defer on a school like Harvard?" Mom wonders aloud.

"Ugh—Mom. We've already talked about this."

"I'm just asking!" She looks at the wall behind me. "You know, when your dad wanted to do this thing with the wallpaper? I was so against it. We fought about it for weeks."

"Why?"

She sighs. "I don't know. It was silly but I was worried he was going to influence you too heavily to be a photographer. It's such a risky business. I don't want you to have to struggle the way we did because we both had such unstable jobs."

"How did he finally convince you?"

"He didn't. He just did it." She looks at the wall, at Dad. "I'm glad."

• • •

In the afternoon, while I'm going through my photos from last night for the millionth time (OK mostly staring at the ones of Dylan), he texts.

Dylan: Ding! Thank you for saving me from what's obv. v. bad ice cream. A bit dramatic but I'm impressed by ur dedication to cause. (U OK?)

Me: Scoops ice cream actually v. good. Just me that's crazy. Sorry.

Dylan: I like crazy. I like u. So u feeling better?

Me: Yes.

Dylan: Good! Liam Argyle photo exhibit at Train Station tomorrow night. 1 night only. Inspiration break? Burgers & shakes at BRGR first?

Dace hands me a blue and white polka dot Kate Spade cosmetics bag on Thursday morning. "What's this?" It's filled with unopened makeup— mascara, two eyeliners, three lipglosses, a creamy M.A.C blush Dace swears by, and a couple of nail polishes.

"Not that you need it, but just a little something for tonight. Just because."

I hug her tight. "Love you." I put the bag in my locker, and my phone buzzes in my back pocket.

Mom: Dace's mom is trying to reach her. Tell her to answer her phone.

I show the phone to Dace. She groans.

"Someone stole my mom's iPad," Dace says.

"What? Are you sure?"

121

"Positive. Vivs reamed me out this morning when she couldn't find it. I told her I haven't seen it but she says that it was on her nightstand when they left for Vegas. She thinks I brought it to school—so I went with that, to buy some time, but I don't even know why, because I haven't touched the thing. I don't know what I'm going to do. She's going to kill me if I don't get it back from whoever stole it."

"Who would steal it?"

"Well, someone who was in the house. We've got to figure out who that chick was that was making out with Cole. It's got to be her."

"I guess . . ." I say. "But what about Cole or Asher, if they were in the house?"

"Well, if we're going down the boytoy route, what about Ben . . ." she says, warningly.

"But he was with me the whole time," I say, feeling a strange defensiveness.

"Fuck."

"—tional," I say out of habit.

She glares at me. "I wish we knew who the girl was. That's it, I'm calling him." She punches Cole's number into her phone. "Of course, no answer. Screening my calls. Ugh. Ass."

"—phixiation."

"*Really* not in the mood, Pippa."

"Sorry. Maybe his phone's off. He could be in class."

Dace groans. "Blonde hair . . . let's think."

"Caitlyn. Elaine. Jade. Vanessa," I say.

Dace rattles off a few more: "Lauren. Emi."

"I think we need to make a list." I grab a binder

from my locker and flip to the back where there are blank pages.

IPAD THEFT SUSPECTS
Ben (but he was with me the whole time)
Cole (too preoccupied with girl he was with?)
Random girl who hooked up with Cole (Need to narrow down list to fewer than 17 possible blondes)
Gemma (no way—we've been friends with Gemma since sixth grade)
Emma (see "Gemma")
Asher (doesn't make sense since he doesn't go to Spalding, so not connected to other stolen items)
Pippa (obviously not)
Dace (see "Pippa")

"This is why we made the no-one-gets-in-the-house rule," Dace groans. "At least we've got a short list, I guess."

"Of no one who did it. Which means it's probably someone we didn't know who got in."

"But how?"

"Same way Cole and that girl got in." I shrug. "Did we leave a door open? Did someone find the spare key?"

Dace leans back against her locker. "What are we going to do?"

"*Hall Pass* comes out tomorrow. You can show your mom that there's been a bunch of thefts, especially of electronics, and then she'll know it's not really your fault. It was circumstantial," I offer, but she shakes her head.

"No offense, Pip, but an article isn't going to do me any good. What I need is an iPad. I have to replace my mom's. Can you go in on it with me?"

I laugh but then I realize from the look on her face that she isn't joking.

"I don't even have a job, Dace. Or an allowance. Why don't you just tell your mom the truth? Seriously, it's not your fault."

"You don't get it. Not only was I not allowed to have a party, I was supposed to be at that Cheektowaga car show. If my mom finds out I bailed on it and lied about it too, she's going to kill me."

"Wait, what? The car show was last weekend? Why didn't you go?"

She looks at me, exasperated. "Because, Pippa . . ." and she looks like she's going to cry.

I go to hug her but she pulls away. "I had a go-see for *Marie Claire*," she says. "That's why."

"You did? That's incredible. When did this happen?" Why didn't she tell me earlier? I try to replay the last few days to figure out when Dace and I weren't together.

She shrugs. "It's no big deal."

"It's a *huge* deal."

"You know what?" Dace says, slamming her locker. "It's fine. I'll just use the money I made at my last shoot to buy the iPad. No big deal."

● ● ●

Dace is sitting in the caf with a bunch of seniors she used to play basketball with. I sit down, putting my tray of fries and chocolate milk on the table. She reaches over and picks up a fry, then breaks off tiny pieces before putting them in her mouth.

"Can you eat the whole thing?" I say grumpily.

She grabs another, pops it in her mouth, chews it and spits it into a napkin.

"That's disgusting."

"You know what's disgusting? Muffin tops." She contorts herself to check out the back fat above the top of her jeans. Back fat that does not exist.

"You do not have a muffin top."

"Not yet. But that's because I just spit out that fry. Trust me, it's what all models do. That or cocaine. Do you want me to develop a coke habit?"

"I want you to eat."

"I am." She reaches into her bag and pulls out a Sugar-Free Red Bull and a plastic bag of celery. "Did you know it burns more calories to chew celery than it actually has?"

"That's called negative energy. And likely also a form of eating disorder."

"Hilarious, *Mom.*"

"What's wrong with you?" I ask before I can stop myself. Dace gives me a death stare.

"I'm sorry," I concede. "I'm stressed about Vantage Point."

"Why?"

"Nothing . . . never mind," I say, but I can't think of any way to cover, and Dace knows I'm lying.

"Spill it."

"I changed my theme," I say so quietly I can barely hear myself.

"When? To what?"

"It's just—I got this idea to do something else . . . It's about memory. Memories. I was inspired and just sort of playing around with it—and it—it's just sort of worked out."

"Memories?" Dace says. "That's the name? Like the corners of my mind?"

"Are you making fun of me?"

"It's just so brilliant. I hear literal is back this year."

"It has nothing to do with you." Why is she making this all about her when this has *nothing* to do with her? Who cares if she's the subject of my photos? It's my *photos* that matter.

"How long ago did you decide this?"

"A while ago. And you can't be upset with me. You don't let me tag along to any shoots. What was I supposed to take pictures of?" It's a low blow, since not tagging along to shoots really isn't the reason I changed themes.

"When were you planning to tell me, ever?" She bites into a celery stick as if my answer won't matter to her.

I tell her that of course I was planning to tell her, but I didn't know how and I didn't want her to misunderstand.

"Misunderstand what? That you think I'm not good enough to be the model in your photos? That you can't win with me in them? Thanks for your support."

"Support? I didn't complain that you're not bringing me to your shoots, did I? No, because whether you bring me or not doesn't affect your career. Why can't you do the same for me?"

"Ha! If you hadn't been so self-absorbed, maybe you'd notice that I'm not *going* to shoots. But you haven't, because everything is All About Pippa, All the Time. Even right now. This is all about you. So fine, let's make this about you and your *new theme*. Take a picture of this." She gives me a smirk. "A memory of when I used to be your best friend."

● ● ●

As though I need one more thing to do, I get to spend the afternoon at the hospital because even though I'm not supposed to work Thursdays, next Monday is Columbus Day and blah blah blah volunteers can't work on holidays, we have to make up the hours and I got stuck with today. Which totally sucks because on top of everything else, the last thing I need, three days before Vantage Point when I'm still not finished my entry, and on the same afternoon that I get in the fight of all fights with my best friend, is to add in a little Sunny McSunshine time at the hospital. Argh!

Even Hannah senses I'm distracted.

"Why don't you take one of the patients for a walk?" she suggests when she sees me watering the plant at the reception desk. The water is filled to the rim and overflowing onto the counter.

I head down the hall to Dorothy's room because

I know she'll be up for it. Today she's wearing mint green elastic-waist pants and an argyle sweater. She's totally ready for the shuffleboard circuit.

"I like your outfit," I tell her as we walk.

"I've had this outfit since 1972. You know I haven't gained one pound since I was 21?" She laughs.

"That's impressive."

"Not really. Sure, when I was your age, it was great. Now it hurts to sit on hard chairs."

I laugh. "Because of the hip replacement?"

"No, I'm too skinny!"

"You should eat more ice cream," I say.

"I can't have dairy. I really miss ice cream," she says.

"Me too," I say, thinking about Scoops. And Dylan.

We turn the corner and start down the next hallway. "When do you think you'll get out of here?"

"Who knows? On top of the iron hip, I've got a heart arrhythmia they're monitoring."

"Don't you wish you could go home?"

"Well, I do miss playing bridge with my friends. Thursdays are bridge days at the retirement home, and that Eleanor"—she shakes her head—"she is going to gloat like no one's business if she wins because I'm not there. Other than that, I don't mind the break. I've read four Harlequins since I got here. In the middle of *The Mistress's Secret Baby* right now. Jake just found out that Carolyn's baby is actually his." Her eyes widen. "Besides, being here gives me hope."

"Hope?"

"Sure," Dorothy says, leaning on the railing for a moment. "That they'll figure out what's wrong with my heart. If I weren't here, who knows what could've happened. Good thing I broke my hip, I say. I want to see my grandchildren graduate."

"How old are they?" An orderly passes us, pushing an empty gurney.

"Twelve and fourteen. So I've gotta keep this thing ticking for a while." She pats her chest and we continue down the hall. "Listen, don't you worry about me. Now, my turn. I wanted to ask you something. Could you help me with my makeup?"

"I'm not very good at makeup, actually," I confess, thinking of Dace. Constantly giving me makeup tips, even though I rarely wear more than mascara and lipgloss. Then I remember the makeup bag Dace gave me.

"I saw the way you were looking at me the other day. I know you can do a better job than I can. At least you can *see* what you're doing."

● ● ●

Dorothy sits in the chair by the window. With the curtains pulled back, there's a ton of natural light. The brand new mascaras, liners and lipsticks are lined up on the windowsill. I pull up the other chair so I'm facing her.

I stand in front of her, channeling Dace. Starting with eyeshadow, so you can wipe off any mistakes. Then eyeliner. Dorothy's eyelids are wrinkled, and it's hard to make a straight line, but I don't let on.

"Look down," I prompt. Her blonde lashes turn black with mascara.

Dorothy sits patiently through it all. "Now it's time for the lips," I say, looking at my choices for lip color. "The trick for lips is to use a lipliner first. The problem is, there's all those hideous dark ones—it's better to use one the same shade as your actual lip color."

Dorothy nods seriously, taking it all in. "See this one?" I hold up a light pinkish-beige lipliner. "This is pretty good for you." I trace her lips with the pencil as I'm talking. "You've got to stay on the lips, not outside. Then, when you put lipstick or lipgloss on, it'll stay inside the lines. It's like coloring."

I fill in her lips with one of her lipsticks, then use my finger to add a dab of my clear gloss overtop. I study Dorothy. "I think we're done. But you tell me what you think." I stand, grabbing my camera from the bed. "Can I take your picture?" I want to show Dace—that is, if Dace and I ever talk again. I adjust the shutter speed to use the natural light, then start snapping Dorothy from various angles.

"What do you think?" I say a while later, pulling the empty chair beside her and sitting down again. She leans in as I scroll through the pictures for her. When we reach the end, I look at her. There are tears in her eyes.

I lean over and give her a hug. Her ribs make ridges in her back, and I try not to squeeze too hard, but I can feel that she's squeezing me with all her strength.

She dabs at her eyes with a tissue. "My mascara's going to run," she says, and I laugh.

The clock at the nurses' station says 6:20. Just enough time to change. Orange stretchy skirt, black leggings, tan cable-knit sweater, handful of bangles. The new pink lipgloss Dace gave me makes me happy and sad at once.

Once I'm out the front doors, I check my phone. 6:30. I don't see Dylan's dad-mobile anywhere.

6:35: I debate texting him.

6:40: Text him to tell him I'm waiting out front, on the front steps, in case I made a mistake about where we were supposed to meet. Like, helicopter pad on the roof?

6:41: Stare at my phone.

6:42: Still staring.

6:43: Oh my god. He's standing me up.

6:44: Send myself a text to make sure my phone's working.

6:45: Phone dings! Text! My heart starts to beat faster. Then realize: it's from me.

6:46: Turn my phone off. Then back on. Then off. Then on.

6:47: Almost throw my phone against the wall but decide against it.

6:48: Think of very bad things that may have happened to him. Five-car pileup. Hijacking. Wonder if I should walk through Emergency to see if he's lying on a stretcher, waiting to get admitted after being in a hit-and-run accident.

Back inside, the atrium's empty, so I walk down the hall to the cafeteria instead of the ER. Callie's on cash. My hands are sweating.

"Hey Callie."

She looks up from her magazine. "Hey, what's up?" she says with a smile.

"Have you seen Dylan?"

She shakes her head. "Not in a while. Why? Everything OK?" She looks genuinely concerned.

Do I tell her we have a date? But then tell her he's standing me up? "I'm just worried because he hasn't texted."

"I'm sure he has a good excuse," Callie says, ringing in a doctor's order. "I just . . . Dylan is a great guy. But you shouldn't have really high expectations of him."

High expectations? All I had was the expectation that if we made a plan, we were actually sticking to it. Or if not, that the person canceling might send a text. Is that too much to ask?

"I . . . I think you might be wanting more from Dylan than he can give you right now."

She takes a 10 from the doctor, and then gives him a handful of change. As he walks away, she looks at me. "You know what? I've already said too much."

●　●　●

Ben Baxter is eating frozen pizza with my mother when I come home. WTF?

"Hey babe," he says, getting up and wiping his mouth with a napkin. I am literally struck dumb, and it lasts long enough for him to walk over and kiss me on the cheek. Like we've been dating for years.

"Look who's here," Mom says. "I told him you were

at the photo exhibit, but he hadn't eaten. So I insisted he stay. At least somebody likes my pizza offerings." She grins. "Did you eat? Are you hungry? How was the exhibit? You're home earlier than I expected."

"I didn't go. Long story."

"You still want to catch it?" Ben asks.

I look at the clock. Already after 8. "It closes at 9," I say.

"Have you seen me drive?" he asks, then looks back at my mom. "Kidding."

Fifteen minutes later Ben Baxter is through the doors of the Train Station when I realize I haven't been inside since the time with Dad. I throw my camera in front of my face, focusing the frame on the old steel doors, and breathe. Snap a few pics. Then head in. Panic attack averted.

"There's only 20 minutes left," the woman at the desk tells us as Ben throws down some money but he just waves her off and grabs my hand. Unlike Dylan's, Ben's hands are super soft.

Forget about him! Dylan stood me up. Ben is here. I squeeze his hand.

Liam Argyle's photos are so good they make me anxious at first, like I'll never be that good, so now on top of obsessing about being here, and Dylan, I'm stressing about my future. But then, Argyle's style consumes me. The way he both employs and breaks rules gets me thinking about new ways to shoot. A photograph of a row of street lamps catches my eye. It's shot in black and white and the lamps are glowing, all but one, in the dark sky. There's something about the photo . . .

"Does this one look familiar to you?" I ask Ben, and he looks at it and shrugs. "Naw," he says, pulling me toward the next print. The PA system announces the gallery's closing. Ben grabs my hand, but I shake my head.

The photos he showed, at his first photo club meeting.

"Don't *you* have a photo like this?" I ask.

"Could be," he says. "Who can remember every photo they've ever taken?"

We drive home in silence and when we turn onto my street, he pulls over to the curb.

"I've got to get home," I say, as he unbuckles his seatbelt.

"Come on," he coaxes, his left hand on the back of my neck, pulling me into him. My stomach churns. He leans in and kisses me.

I want to tell him he's not my boyfriend. That I don't like him that way. Who can remember every photo they've ever taken? I can. There's an iPhoto album in my brain where every single one is collated and tagged, easy for me to call up—the composition, the thinking process, the set-up and capture. And I'd certainly remember a shot like the one Ben Baxter showed me. Any *real* photographer would. It's a great photo. So: was it a coincidence? An homage to Liam Argyle? Or did he just rip it off?

His face is smooth, but it might as well be sandpaper. His breath smells like peppermint, but it might as well be rotten eggs. His tongue pushes past my lips with too much saliva, and I last maybe 10 seconds before I can't stand another second more.

Mr. Winters wins the award for slowest walker, but he gets away with it, on account of being about 42 pounds and 93 years old and having tubes sprouting out of the most random places. "I know *I'm* slow, but what's your excuse?" he says. He's right. He may be shuffling, but I'm the one who's dragging my feet. I'm supposed to be accompanying Mr. Winters on his way to the cancer center, just like I accompanied my dad. But ever since Dad, I made a rule, and right now, I'm breaking it.

PIPPA'S RULES ABOUT GOING TO THE
CANCER CENTER
  1. Avoid at all cost.

At first, visiting Dad wasn't so bad. Cancer. I didn't even know what the word *meant* then. The first couple of days at the hospital it actually was kind of fun. Mom hung out with him all day, every day, so by the time I showed up after school she was ready to head home for a bit, for a break. It was tough to get my dad by himself before that. He worked a lot, in his makeshift studio in the basement and in the evenings he often was out meeting with potential clients, like couples who wanted engagement, wedding or maternity photos. But at the hospital, I got him all to myself. He'd save the best part of his lunch for me, the chocolate pudding, and I'd eat it while doing my homework. Then we'd talk about school, about photography, about whatever book I was reading for English class. At first I looked forward to visiting him.

Then the radiation treatments started. Monday through Friday. Sometimes Mom would take him, but sometimes he was scheduled in the afternoon, and it was me. They didn't take long—the actual treatment was, like, two minutes, but there was some waiting around for his turn—and then we'd be back in his room. The first few weeks were no big deal at all. Sometimes I even forgot he was sick. He didn't seem sick—he was taking enough pills for the pain—and there weren't any real side effects from the radiation. Everyone else always was so bright and cheerful and positive—like he was actually getting better. Like we were winning. I believed it. He was *so* positive. But the signs were all there. He was an in-patient. If he was getting better, why wouldn't they just let him go home between treatments? Because he wasn't getting better. He was getting worse.

And it all happened so quickly once he started chemo. He got all puffy. His skin was blotchy. Every time he got up to go to the bathroom or whatever he'd leave a tiny clump of hair on his pillow. One of his fingernails fell off. You hear about how fingernails and hair are made out of the same stuff, but you don't really *get* it until you're playing Go Fish with a dad whose forefinger nail fell off the day before and who has half the hair he did two weeks ago. I could see it in my mom's face too. We weren't winning anymore, and the nurses' cheer started to seem, like, obscene. *Good afternoon?* Seriously?

A couple of years back, maybe when I was 13 or so, I had a friend—well, she was a Facebook friend, not an IRL friend—and her brother had leukemia and she would mention it in her status updates. "Just three more chemo sessions left!" There was something heroic about her positivity and maybe I was a bit jealous of her—no, not of her, I was jealous of the opportunity that she had. To be heroic. Everybody talked about her—about how strong she was. I wrote a few Facebook status updates like that, and I knew people were talking about me. I felt special. I was the girl whose dad had cancer.

And then, when I realized I was about to become the girl whose dad died of cancer, I stopped feeling anything at all.

It was like that YouTube video that guy made a few years ago where he shot a photo of his son every day for 18 years, and then stitched them together into a video? In the span of three minutes, you saw his son grow up. With my dad it was kind of the opposite. Every day Dad looked and acted a little different from the day before. One day he could still walk down the hallway to the vending machines. We'd play a game to see who could put their money in and get their chocolate bar out first. And then, a few days later, he couldn't make it all the way there. And then he couldn't walk at all. And then he couldn't even get out of bed. And then he couldn't go to the bathroom. And then he could barely see, because this thick, milky glaze had formed over his eyes. And then I never saw his eyes again.

As we pass the elevator bank, the doors open. Dylan. "Hey," he says, stepping off the elevator.

"Hi," I say.

What do you say to the guy who totally brushed you off?

"Can you talk for a minute?" he asks, but I shake my head.

"Mr. Winters has chemo. No time to talk." One foot in front of the other, I tell myself, but my legs feel heavy. Please don't give out on me. But then, I feel them start to spaghetti-fy. No no no no no no no.

"Can you take him?" my voice wavering. And then, before he can even react, everything starts to go gray, and then I feel my legs give out beneath me and every-thing goes black like I've closed my eyes, but I don't think I have, because I can't get them to open.

I drop to the floor.

"Hey hey hey hey hey hey," Dylan says softly, dropping down beside me. "You're OK." His arms are around my shoulders, holding me tight.

"Please," I moan.

"I'm not leaving you."

"Pleeeeeeease . . ."

And then his arms leave me. And I shut my eyes tight and focus on my breathing. And block out everything else.

When I open my eyes, it's dark. There's a mop beside me. I blink, adjusting to the dim light, and see that Dylan is in front of me.

"Hey," he says. "Yeah, we're in the supply closet. I didn't want you to become gurney roadkill out in the hallway. So, second time you've fainted with me. I'm starting to worry about the effect I have on you. Every guy wants the ladies to swoon, but this is a bit much," he jokes.

I give a half smile.

"Seriously, you OK?" He puts a hand on my knee.

"Panic attacks."

"Didn't think of that one. From what?"

"I can't handle people with cancer."

"Really?" Dylan says.

"On account of the dying."

"Not everyone dies."

"Eventually they do," I say.

"Eventually everyone dies," Dylan says, then stands up. "Let's get you a drink." He helps me up. His hands are warm.

"What happened to Mr. Winters?" I say as we open the door into the hall, the bright fluorescent lighting making me blink.

"Not to worry—I convinced Ashley to take him. Wasn't difficult. Got her out of sheet-changing duty. It was win-win."

We walk to the elevators, then take them down to the main floor, to the cafeteria. Dylan steers me toward the doors to the pond, telling me he'll be back in a second. I sit by the pond edge, grateful for the fresh air.

Dylan comes back with an apple juice and sits down beside me. His eyes are so warm. When he smiles they crinkle at the edges. Then I remember he ditched me. I'm about to tell him I should get going.

"Listen, I really owe you an apology," Dylan says, handing me the apple juice. "There's no excuse for not showing up last night." He looks apologetic. Actually he looks so apologetic he looks sick. "This sounds so lame, but it's the truth," Dylan says, looking me right in the eyes. Why does he have to be so irresistible? "I was feeling tired, and I thought if I had a quick nap I could shake it off and be on my game with you but I fell asleep and I didn't wake up until this morning. I swear it's the truth. I feel really, really terrible about it. This is totally in the top 10 list of things I feel shitty about doing."

"You have a list?"

He shrugs. "Let me make it up to you?"

"The exhibit was only one night, remember? I went with a friend."

He sighs. "Some other way? Lifetime supply of greasy cheese fries? I'm really, really sorry . . . How was it?"

"Good. I thought it'd be hard to go back to the Train Station. The last time I went to an exhibit there was with my dad."

"That must've been hard. But you did it?"

"Yeah. Maybe I was so preoccupied with everything—you standing me up, and then going after all. But it was OK."

"These past few months for you—I can't even imagine."

"Surreal, maybe? Especially being back here. You know my dad was supposed to shoot the hospital as a project? And then he got sick. Every day it was something else. His body was just shutting down, but it was happening so fast, it was hard to really register what was going on. And then, one day, he just . . . didn't wake up.

"Like seriously, the next day we were at the funeral home, deciding on a casket and wording for the obituary, and readings for the funeral, and it just seemed so trivial. Like, what's the point? He's dead. What does *he* care, you know? We're doing it for all these people—these people who *think* they know him."

Dylan's silent, waiting for me to go on.

"I just wanted to wear black. You know, in the movies they wear black. Turns out I didn't own a single black dress. My mom was like, 'Just wear any dress.' But I didn't want to wear *any* dress. I wanted to wear a black dress, like you're supposed to. I couldn't even get that right. I remember standing in my closet looking at my clothes, knowing that whatever I chose I'd never wear again."

"I remember your dress, actually," Dylan says. "Navy with small flowers."

My eyes tingle. "I—I saw you," I say, then ask the question I'd wanted to ask for a long time. "Dylan—why did you come?"

He shrugs. "I don't know. I just . . . I always liked you. I mean, I know I didn't really know you, but . . . it seemed like the right thing to do. My uncle died a few years ago and it made me feel good to see my friends there, even though they didn't even know him."

"How did your uncle die?"

"Motorcycle accident. Right on impact. I was pretty wrecked for a while—we were pretty close. Anyway, I remember thinking how well you were holding it together at your dad's funeral. That couldn't have been easy."

I force a laugh. "I think I was in shock. I didn't know it, but I guess . . . that's the only explanation. You know, we went to the funeral home beforehand. My mom said we'd have one more chance to say goodbye. The previous two nights we'd had these viewings—where people come and look at him, there in the casket, and then stand around making stupid small talk and eating these stale store-bought cookies—you know, the ones with the sugar on top?

"But the day of the funeral was just going to be the three of us. Me, Mom, Dad. Only when we got there the casket was closed. Mom said it was to get him ready to transport to the church, but she didn't tell me. She knew and she didn't tell me that's how it was going to be. I wanted to see him, I wanted to talk to him, not some wooden box." I bite my lower lip. "I wanted to *see* him," I say again. "I didn't get a chance. That was it. What I thought was my chance, totally gone. And then we had to go to the church and listen to some guy talk about my dad and he didn't know him. He called him Ivan. His name is Evan and he called him Ivan."

Dylan lets out a low whistle.

"Oh, the best part?" I say sarcastically. "They played Pachelbel's Canon."

"I don't get it."

"They're constantly pumping that through the cancer ward. It's supposed to be therapeutic or something, and actually it's a really pretty song, and I get it. But my dad heard that song every fucking day. And all it tells you is 'Oh hey, remember? You have cancer. You're gonna die.' He was finally done with all those useless treatments, and what do they play? That fucking song."

The lily pads are starting to brown around the edges. Did I say too much? I've never told anyone how I really felt about that day. Not even Mom. Not even Dace.

"Wow. And then what? You're just supposed to go back to life as normal?"

"Yeah, I guess. Everyone bringing over muffins and casseroles to fill our freezer, and flowers everywhere, like 'Here! Sorry you don't have a dad, but wow, look at all the carnations you've got! Oh and P.S. they're gonna die too. Sucker!'"

"Did you at least get to eat a lot of ice cream? If I had really known you, I would've brought you tons and tons of ice cream."

I shake my head.

"What? No ice cream? Wait, is *that* why you fainted at Scoops? You hate ice cream and I never knew. I'm the worst—"

"No. But I don't go to Scoops anymore."

"And I take you there on our first date? Wow, I suck."

"You didn't know. And I do like ice cream."

"Should we get ice cream now then? Do over? Those mangled ice-cream sandwiches they have in the freezer in the caf? They're always totally deformed, but man, are they addictive."

"I should actually get going," I say, though ice cream with Dylan is totally tempting. "There's one more shot I want for my Vantage Point entry."

"Can I tag along?"

"It's not exactly the most uplifting location. The cemetery."

"I'll take you."

"I haven't been back since the funeral."

"Will you let me go with you?"

It's nice to be asked things. Unlike certain other people, or more accurately, *Ben,* who makes me feel like a passenger in my own life. "I'd like to go with you," I say to Dylan, and it's true, I would. As we're walking back toward the elevators, he stops at the stairwell. "Wait—I have something for you. It's just silly but . . ." He pushes open the door to the stairwell. "Meet me in the atrium in two minutes?" He starts up the stairs, the metal door closing slowly and I wonder where he's going.

But a few minutes later he walks toward me, where I'm sitting at the fountain. He's holding a bunch of Twizzlers tied together at the base with a ribbon, like a bouquet of flowers. "I wanted to give these to you last night. They're probably kind of stale now."

How can I be mad at someone who makes me a bouquet of Twizzlers?

"How'd you know I love Twizzlers?"

Dylan's looking at me with such a hopeful expression. My stomach flips.

"I took a guess. Remember that day in the caf?"

He grins.

"How could I forget? The tissue up my nose. Mortifying."

"Charming, more like it. Maybe I'm biased by my own creativity, but I think this bouquet breaks the Food Theory. Because this looks pretty awesome, and I've had my share of Twizzlers, and they taste good too. So what gives? Have I found the one item in the world that defies that theory?"

I laugh. "You're crazy."

The front doors slide open, the afternoon sun making me squint. I'm about to ask him where he parked when I spot a black SUV. Ben appears around its side, a massive bouquet of flowers in hand.

"What's wrong?" Dylan asks.

Ben waves.

"Do you know that guy?" Dylan says, nodding in Ben's direction.

Ben comes toward me. "Hey babe," he says, kissing me square on the lips before I have a chance to stop him.

"What are you doing here?" I say, then look at Dylan, who's looking at the two of us. I can't read his expression. But I'm not optimistic.

"What, I'm not allowed to come pick up my girl? Hey bro," he adds, nodding at Dylan.

"It's Dylan," Dylan says, studying Ben.

"These are for you," Ben says, thrusting the flowers into my arms, where they dwarf the Twizzlers.

Surely Dylan must know that I wouldn't have told him all that stuff about Dad if he was just some guy? Surely he can see Ben's not my type? But Dylan is stone faced.

"Got it," he says. "I didn't realize you had a boy-friend. See you, Pippa."

It's the first time he's ever called me by my nick-name. My stomach feels like it's dropped down to my knees. I can't move my legs. Dylan heads toward his car. He ducks behind a cargo van, and he's gone.

"What are those?" Ben says, nodding at the Twizzlers in my hand.

"Twizzlers," I say. "Duh." We look at each other a moment. "Ben—"

But he interrupts me. "I'm going to the mall to get the stuff for my Vantage Point display," he says. "You want to come?"

He means those three-panel foam project boards that everyone uses to display their photos. I need one too. "Actually, I guess I do."

And that's how I end up in Ben Baxter's SUV, headed to the mall, of all places. I touch my phone about a half-dozen times during the ride over, con-sidering what to text Dylan. But I have to forget about my so-called love life. I have to focus. I have to finish my Vantage Point entry.

● ● ●

But I can't. When we get to the mall I tell Ben I'm going to run off to use the bathroom. On the way I pass a large setup of chairs in front of a stage that has a T-shaped runway. The lights dim just as I get there. It seems like ages ago that Dace was in one of these fashion shows—brief exhibitions of mall clothes that happen every hour, on the hour, to remind shoppers of the wonderful products available to buy. Beats pump from the oversized black speakers on either side of the stage. The black curtains part and the first model walks out.

It's Dace.

She walks the length of the runway, pauses at the end, turns in that way I've seen her practice a million times, and struts back to the top of the stage before disappearing through the curtain. I grab my phone.

Me: Hey! I'm here at your show. You look great! Meet me after?

She doesn't answer my text but she obviously doesn't have time. Dace comes out a few more times, and I wave, but she never makes eye contact. The lights are bright—maybe she can't see me? The show ends and she still hasn't texted so I wait by the side of the stage. Eventually, all the models come out to see their friends or parents. Everyone except Dace. There's a black makeshift tent behind the stage, where the models change. "Dace?" I push open the curtains but the space is empty.

My phone buzzes and my heart skips. Dylan?

Dace? But it's Ben. Of course it's Ben. Wondering where I am. I make my way to the food court.

Ben's at a table for four by the new recycling station. "What happened?" On the chair next to him is a large black board and his satchel, the strap from his camera dangling out the top.

"Dace was in the fashion show." I check my phone but there's no response. And I realize: I still haven't texted Dylan.

"I've still got to use the bathroom—can you just wait with our stuff here a minute?"

"Sure," he says. "Take your time."

Me: BEN IS NOT MY BOYFRIEND!!!!

Me: I don't have a boyfriend!

Me: Can we talk?

When I get back Ben's just leaving the Sbarro a few steps from our table. He sets down a tray of Diet Pepsis and pizza slices. I reach for the Canon Rebel on the table and he says, "That's mine, babe." He's right—there's no dent on the case. "And listen, no more pictures right now. Eat up. I've got to get going." But I haven't even gotten my foam board yet.

The pizza tastes like the cardboard box in my mouth. I wipe my hands on a napkin and stand up. He hands me my camera and bag, and I distractedly sling them over my body. "I'm going to take the bus home—I still have to get my foam board."

Ben shrugs, and then I go for it. "Listen, Ben, we need to talk." My heart pounds. I've never done this before. "I don't think this is going to work between us. I really like you, but I just don't think I like you in that way."

Ben keeps his eyes on the pizza. "Because of that dude?"

"Yes. No. It's complicated."

"Huh. Well that sucks. But . . . all right." He doesn't actually seem that heartbroken. "See you at Vantage Point?"

"I'll see you tomorrow, won't I? Mrs. Edmonson wants everyone in photo club to meet at the school. To look at our contest entries."

"Sure," he says. "Right. See you tomorrow."

• • •

The house is quiet when I get home. I head straight upstairs to my room. I plug my camera into my computer, and check my phone again as the pictures download. Still nothing. Once the pictures have finished downloading I pull them up one at a time.

My heart pounds. Something's off. The pictures are different. They're shots of kids at school, shots of football practice, shots of some SUV. Ben's SUV. I pull the cord from the camera and look at the pics through the screen. Same pics. I turn the camera over in my hands. My hands are shaking. The dent. There's no dent.

This isn't my camera.

My hands can't text fast enough.

Me: I have your camera. Where r u? Can u
drop it off?

Ben: Really? Weird. At a party. Camera's in
my car. I'll drop off tomorrow?

Me: I really need it tonight—I want to finish
my VP entry!!!

No response.
I squint at the screen. Wait, what?
My Vantage Point folder is gone.
Hands shaking, I call Mom.
"Were you on my computer?" I ask, panicked.
"Of course not. What's wrong?"
"My Vantage Point folder is gone. Trash is empty.
Someone's been on my computer."
"Breathe, Pippa," she says, then gasps.
"What?"
"I don't want to jump to any conclusions, but
when Ben was over, he asked if he could get a photo
from your computer—one of the two of you he said
you took awhile back. He wanted to get it printed
and framed as a gift for you."
I feel sick.
"I'm so sorry, Pip. He wanted it to be a surprise
and I thought it was so sweet of him. Do you think
he deleted your photos by mistake?"
He didn't delete them by mistake. He did it on
purpose. Talk about keeping your enemies closer.

• • •

Hours later I'm in bed, tossing and turning, when my phone buzzes. I grab it from under my pillow, praying it's Ben.

Dace: Hekp.

Me: ???

Dace. Help! Can u come get me?

Me: Where r u?

Dace: Cole's. Crazy party. 47 Oakwood. Or Maplewood? A street with a tree name.

Dace: Please get me? Drunk. PS Sorry.

Me: Be there in 5.

My hoodie's by the bedside table and I pull it over the clothes I fell asleep in. The bedroom door makes its usual creak, but Mom's still snoring as I pass her room.

I tiptoe down the stairs and out the back door, then make my way around to the front, pop the car in neutral and back it out of the driveway. It's in a case like this that I'm glad we don't have a garage. There's no way I could escape undetected if I had to open a garage door.

For a split second I feel a pang of guilt over Mom's

rule about driving without a licensed driver, which is, in a nutshell, don't, since it's illegal. But then I make my own rule.

PIPPA'S RULES FOR BREAKING MOM'S
RULES ABOUT DRIVING
1. When your best friend drunk texts that she needs rescuing even when you're technically in a fight, drive the car.

When I get to Cole's house, bass is pumping out the windows. The street is lined with cars, but there's a spot at the far end of the street. Once I'm inside, the smoke in the house requires actual effort to penetrate. People are everywhere—dancing, making out, passed out. How will I find Dace?

Me: I'm here. Where r u?

Dace: Upstairs. Bathroom.

Strange kids crowd the staircase in a line that leads all the way to bathroom. At least, it does in those '80s movies.

"Hey, there's a line," a guy hollers as I push past him on the stairs.

"Yeah, well, I'm cutting it," I grumble, totally focused. "Dace?" I pound on the door.

It opens a crack and a hand grabs mine and pulls me inside.

Dace is a mess. Her eyeshadow is smudged and her mascara runs down her cheeks. Her eyes are bloodshot. She smells like she's been bathing in rum.

"They were all doing coke and they wanted me to do it and . . ."

Whoa. I pull her into me. "Did you?"

She shakes her head. "That's why I'm hiding in the bathroom."

She wants to escape out the bathroom window but it's like a 40-foot drop to the grass below. I grab her hand and pull open the bathroom door.

"Ooh, lezzers in the bathroom!" Some guy shouts then makes kissy noises at us. I stifle the impulse to kick him in the balls. It would be too good a fate for him. Instead I pull Dace toward, and then through, the front door.

"My head . . ." Dace moans.

● ● ●

Dace promises to be quiet as I open the door to the house, and somehow we manage to get upstairs without waking Mom. I go to the bathroom and get the bottle of Advil.

She is spread out across my bed. I push her over to one side and pull the covers over her, then climb in beside her.

"I love you, Pip."

"I love you too, Dace. I'm sorry."

"Me too. So dumb. Thanks for coming to get me."

"Why were you there? I thought you were done with Cole."

"I don't know. I hate the fact that he hooked up

with some other girl at my party. I wanted to get back at him. Asher broke up with me or whatever, not like we were together, but anyway. So, I don't know, I had this idea I'd make out with Cole's best friend at the party. Get back at him."

"Who? Zach Gellerman? You're so competitive." I hug her. "So did you?"

"Oh who knows? I definitely made out with some guy, but I don't think he even knew Cole. Not that Cole even noticed. Not my proudest moment, that's for sure."

"Oh Dace . . ."

"You know who else was there, sucking face?"

"Who?"

"Ben."

"Really? Shit. I need to get my camera back from him. I'm 99% sure he swapped it on purpose. And deleted all my photos for Vantage Point from my computer."

Dace sits up, eyes wide. "What? Are you kidding?" Then she gasps. "Wait—what if he stole my mom's iPad too?"

I think back to the night at Dace's party—and the way, contrary to what I told Dace before, I left Ben alone while I went to the bathroom. Shit. Bathroom breaks, apparently, are my downfall. Could Ben be the thief of Spalding High?

I groan. "He had the chance to grab your mom's iPad. I'm so sorry."

"I've got an idea," Dace says, and she scrambles out of my bed. "We just need a clothes hanger."

"Cut the engine and turn off the lights," Dace says as we turn onto Oakwood. "Let's coast the rest of the way."

My hands grip the steering wheel, devoid of feeling. "The street's uphill. I'll just park here."

"Pippa! We're, like, five houses away. How are we going to make a quick getaway?"

"We'll run," I say, shutting off the engine and opening the door.

We find the SUV parked across the street from Cole's house—how'd I ever miss it the first time? "Just act normal," I hiss, walking around the front bumper and over to the curb. Turns out that advice was futile. Dace is on all fours, the coat hanger she brought, now stuffed up the back of her hot pink shirt. She nods, motioning for me to join her as she crawls on the grass. She's swaying. Still drunk. Why did I—in my perfectly sober state—let her talk me into this? I pull her to her feet and hold her up as we creep past the cars.

We're steps away from the SUV when Dace breaks free. "All rigggggggght!" she roars like she's a UFC announcer. "Let's bust this guy!"

"Dace—geezus!"

I pull her down to the grass, behind the SUV, so we're out of sight of anyone inside Cole's house. Dace pulls the coat hanger from under her shirt and unwinds the top, then hands it to me. "You're on, Pippa."

The wire ends in a hook. It looks a bit like the question mark floating above my head. The SUV's front window seems impenetrable. "Dace—I don't have a clue how to do this."

Dace throws her hands in the air. "This is your moment, Pippa. Your chance for revenge. Your *opportunity* to get back what's rightfully yours. Also, I'm gonna throw up." She puts her head on the grass, moaning. Her long blonde hair spills over her shoulders.

"Oh crap." I lean over and rub her back. "C'mon, I'll take you home."

Dace lifts her head. "No way. We're not leaving. You slide the hanger between the window and the door and wiggle it around—there's a switch that it has to catch on—or something. It totally worked this one time for Veronica Mars."

My bitten fingernails aren't able to pry the rubber weather sealing away from the SUV's glass window. "Dace, can you do this? Dace? Where are you?"

Smash!

The tinkling of pebbles—glass, actually—spilling against concrete. Oh, there's Dace—standing at the back of the SUV beside a boulder-sized hole in the back window.

My scream's drowned out by the wail of an alarm. The SUV's lights flash. "Run!" Dace yells, sprinting back toward my Honda. But my memory card. The hole the rock made is just big enough. My cheeks press up against the sharp edge of the tinted safety glass. The streetlight shines through the hole and I can see what the tinted glass hid moments ago:

a rear compartment full of electronics. There's an iPad, a couple of iPods and then, by the rear wall of the back seat, the Canon Rebel camera that's the object of this misbegotten quest.

Then comes the blare of a second alarm. It's not coming from the car, but from behind me—and it's getting louder. A glance around the SUV's side, and I can see the lights of oncoming police cars.

There's the old familiar feeling. The creeping black around the edge of my vision. The world tilts—and I clutch at something, anything to stay vertical.

No. No. No. Not now.

Hey, panic attack? You listening? Now's just not a good time. *Anytime* but now.

It's the rear windshield wiper—that's what I'm grabbing. OK. My arm fits through the hole in the window but my hand gropes only air. The vehicle dips when I step onto the rear bumper. I push my arm in up to the shoulder—*there*, the camera strap. The lens knocks out a new section of window on its way out just as two cop cars pull up in front of Cole's house. Noise complaint—that's why they must be here, but they'll register which vehicle the alarm's coming from soon enough. I have seconds, really. Just enough time to grab one more thing before I duck down and scurry back to Mom's Honda.

Dace is huddled down in the passenger seat of the Honda when I get in.

"Did you get it?"

I hand her my camera, and then the second thing the iPad that was alongside it. "It's Vivs's color," Dace says, flipping open the magnetic pink cover and turning it on. The car starts on the first twist of the ignition and I pull the Honda out of the tight space, narrowly missing the back bumper of the car in front of us. "That's what I like to see," Dace says, showing me the picture of Vivs and Fred on the tablet's home screen. "It's hers. You saved the day, Pippa." We're around the corner when Dace sticks her head out the half-opened window.

"Busted, asshole!" she shouts into the night.

Under the circumstances—and that we're out of sight from the cops—I let the swearing-ban violation slide.

Dace's groaning wakes me up the next morning. "My head . . ." she moans, and for a moment I forget about last night. Then I remember everything.

"Adviiiiiiilllll." I get her a glass of water from the bathroom. Thankfully Mom got up early to work the 7 a.m. shift and she obviously didn't even realize Dace was here.

Dace moans some more. "Ohhhhh . . ." she says as I climb back in bed.

"Hey, we didn't talk about the fashion show," I say.

More groaning.

"You got my text."

She nods, running her fingers through the ends of her hair.

"Why'd you sneak away without talking to me?"

She looks at me in disbelief. "That's what you

care about? Not that you *saw me in a mall fashion show?*"

"Of course that was a surprise, but all I care about is our friendship."

"I'm sorry," she mumbles. "I was so embarrassed that you saw me and that I lied to you . . ."

"What's going on?" It's so unlike Dace to be like this. She's usually the strong, confident one.

"Come on," she moans. "I went on and on about how I wasn't doing mall shows anymore because they're the death of any real modeling career and how I'm better than that and I get the new agent and then you catch me in my lie?"

"But I don't get it . . ."

She's staring at the comforter. "I can't *do* anything more than mall shows. That's what the new agent says, just like the old agent said. It's my destiny. Mall model forever . . ." Tears start down her face and she sniffs, still staring at the comforter. Then she starts to cry. Really cry. I've never seen her like this. Tears uncontrollable, face blotchy, black eye makeup smearing down her cheeks. Her nose running and her breath catching. But I get it. Modeling is her life. I can't imagine how I'd feel if someone told me I wasn't talented enough to go to Tisch. But I also don't believe that Dace's career is over. She *is* talented. Surely those two agents don't know everything there is to know. I reach over to hug her. I pull her into me and she buries her head in my chest. I smooth her hair, the way Mom does to me.

"That's not true," I reassure her.

"But it is." Her voice is muffled in my tank top.

"I'm over the hill. And there's nothing else I want to do. I'm going to have to face reality. Live the American Dream and work at the dollar store."

"Just so you know, I'm pretty sure you will never have to work at the dollar store—unless you get hired by a mag for some ironic haute couture shoot in one."

"You don't get it. You're legitimately good at what you love to do. You're going to be a photographer, just like you've always wanted. But I don't have a backup plan."

"Listen to me," I say, handing her a wad of Kleenex. "You don't *need* a backup plan. You're not going to be a model. You *are* a model. We just need a better plan. And we're going to figure it out."

"We are?"

I nod. "And I already know what we're going to do."

"What?" Dace rubs her mascara-smudged eyes.

"I'm going to win that competition—somehow—and get into the Tisch camp. And you're going to come with me and find yourself an agent in New York. One who gets you real go-sees for real jobs. Deal?"

She nods. "Oh, one other thing I should probably mention."

"What? Last night while you were drunk you binged on entire Fudgee-O's rather than tossing the wafers?" I say, pointing to the near-empty bag on the floor. "It's OK. You're allowed."

She shakes her head. "I still have my V-card."

"What?"

"I lied. I don't know why. Asher and I didn't do it. I mean, he wanted to and I sort of wanted to but then he passed out. And when you told me about Cole and how he was fooling around with some random chick—and I actually liked him better than Asher. What an ass. I don't know why I lied. I just felt stupid. And I wanted Cole to hear the Asher rumor somehow, to make him think I didn't care about him—even though I did."

"But why did you lie to me?"

"I don't know. I don't think it really even had anything to do with you. I was just feeling like such a failure about everything and I didn't want to tell you how badly modeling was going because I felt like we had this plan for our lives and I was letting you down. I thought that you'd make it big and you wouldn't need me anymore."

I shake my head. "I'll always need you—whether we're super famous or both working at the dollar store."

"Could you even imagine? Us, at the dollar store?" She giggles, and so do I. Then reality sets in. All my first-choice photos are gone. Maybe I can use alternates from those same shoots. At least I have the ones on my camera . . .

I unplug the charger from the outlet by my desk and pop the battery in my camera. "I took some pics of you in the show. You look really good."

"Ugh," Dace says, but moves to the end of the bed as I turn my camera on and press the playback button. The screen is black.

"Fuck."

"What?" Dace is standing over my shoulder. I flip the power button on and off again, but the screen's still blank. I open the tiny door that holds the data card. It's empty.

"He even stole my data card! I'm screwed."

26 HOURS UNTIL VANTAGE POINT

Everything's so messed up that I even arrive late to my 10 a.m. Vantage Point review session with Mrs. Edmonson. She's booked each of us into 15-minute slots to individually show her our Vantage Point entries and give us feedback before the big day. When I get to the photocopy room, Ben's inside and I can hear Mrs. Edmonson gushing over his photos. The metal lockers are cold against my T-shirted back as I slide down to sit on the tile floor. When he opens the door, I stand up and rush over to him. He looks away.

"Ben—my data card. Please, just give it back."

"I don't know what you're talking about," he says, not even stopping. And he's around the corner.

"Pippa?" Mrs. Edmonson calls from inside the photocopy room. I swallow hard. Push the door open.

She pats to the chair beside her. "Everything OK? You're late—I let Ben go ahead of you because he was waiting."

"Sorry," I say, plugging my USB key into the computer. Focus on the photos. Which are fine. Fine. Fine. Fine. Breathe.

"My theme is Memories," I explain half-heartedly, opening the folder with the photos I'd backed up to my laptop—ones that never made it into the folder he deleted because they weren't my best shots. The gazebo in Hannover Park, the single photo on the yellowed album page, room 334 at the hospital, the steps leading up to St. Christopher's, my dad's Nikon.

As I walk Mrs. Edmonson through the photos, I feel better. Sure, I know I can do better, but these are still pretty good shots. But when I reach the end, she's silent. Not the reaction I was going for. She clasps her hands, resting them in her lap, and studies me. "Pippa, what's going on?"

"What do you mean?"

"I just saw an almost identical slideshow from Ben. What gives?"

He not only stole my photos but *used* them? "How could he use the same photos? What was his theme?"

"Same theme. Most of the same photos. Maybe slightly different angles, but very, *very* close."

"But how could they be his memories? Mrs. Edmonson, these are *my* memories. The room my dad stayed in at the hospital, his old camera he gave me, which is *right here*"—I pull the Nikon out of my bag. "This is insane. Ben stole my data card, he swapped cameras with me. He stole my Vantage Point photos off my computer."

She looks alarmed. Neither of us speaks. She has to believe me. Who would make that up?

"Pippa, this doesn't reflect well on either one of you. It's your word against his. Why would *he* take your photos?" She crosses her legs. "If the Vantage Point judges think either one of you is using photos that aren't your own, you'll both be disqualified. Not to mention how badly it'll reflect on the school." She thinks for a moment, wringing her hands. "I could tell both of you you're not going to Vantage Point at all for this—clearly one of you is lying—but you're both very talented photographers and I don't want to deny you this opportunity. And I know how much going to the Tisch camp means to you." Her tone softens. "So here's what I'm going to ask. You're going to have to come up with brand new photos for the competition. I don't want to see a single photograph even remotely similar to Ben's. I suggest you start from scratch, to be sure."

"Start from scratch? Are you kidding? I've been working on my entry for *months*! How am I going to come up with six *good* new photos by tomorrow? And what about Ben?"

"I'll tell him the same thing. Now I suggest you get out there and start shooting. You don't have much time."

24 HOURS UNTIL VANTAGE POINT

So many headstones. Tall ones, ominous ones. Flat stones, nestled in the grass, that have probably been there for hundreds of years. Which one is his? It's only been three months, but the last day I was here was so crazy, there were so many people and so many cars, that the cemetery where my dad is buried seems like a different place today. Coming out of the meeting with Mrs. Edmonson I just wanted to talk to my dad about what to do, and my first instinct was to go see him in my room. But Mom'll be home by 1. The last thing I want to do is have to relive the morning.

It seems easier to bear, this place, from behind my camera. It's a clear day that we get only rarely in October, and I set up a couple of headstone shots, but my lens keeps getting drawn to the signs of life all around here. Someone's spent the summer going nuts with the Miracle-Gro. Red impatiens contrast with the green of the lawns and the gray of the head-stones. Strange how the thing that pops out of cemetery photos are images of life. I'm so distracted, so in the frame, that I'm taken by surprise when I recognize my dad's name on a monument.

I kneel down in the grass, keeping the camera to my face and focus on the headstone. I zoom in on the pebbled texture of the stone, snap some photos, then slowly zoom out, taking in the headstone against the grass. Then I rest the camera in my lap and fold my legs over so I'm sitting cross-legged on the ground.

"Hi," I say finally. "So . . . this is weird, huh? We never talk here. Which uh, OK, kinda my fault. It's not like you have much choice in the matter. But I just . . . I don't know. I have no good excuse. Pain to get here on the bus? Lame, I know! Like, you died, and you're stuck out here by yourself—or I guess there's other people around but it's not like you know them, right? And I can't be bothered to get on a bus? It's totally not that. I guess it's just . . . Mom comes all the time and I thought, like, maybe in the same way she doesn't know how we talk in my room, maybe she doesn't want me here? Like it's her place to be with you, alone? So don't tell her I came, OK?"

My camera is resting in the space between my crossed legs, and I keep my eyes on the grass that's, I guess, six feet above him.

"You know what I hate?" I continue, grabbing my camera again, and shooting around the headstone. "When we're in my room I can just pretend you're in New York for work. That you got a studio there like you always wanted and you're living the dream. And I'm—just at Dace's or school or whatever when you come home. Like I just missed you. When I go to Tisch camp, we'll hang out for the whole two weeks, just like we used to. I know it's crazy but it's part of why I want to win so badly. But then what? I get there and where are you?"

I wait for Dad to answer, to tell me that it's normal what I'm feeling, or that he's glad I'm here, or that yes, he is actually in New York and we're going to have so much fun when I'm there. *If* I'm there. But he doesn't say anything. I lower the camera again.

Silence. Not my dad's voice, solving my problems for me. Not like I was hoping. I stand up to take it all in. The grass that tops my dad's final resting place. The annual flowers decorating his headstone. Everything but the words.

"I don't think I'm going to Tisch camp, Dad. Remember Vantage Point? The photo contest that was going to be my in to get into Tisch? Memories— that was going to be my theme, but it can't be, not anymore."

I focus on the front of the headstone now, on the words visible above the tall grass, inscribed in stone.

Evan Alexander Greene
July 24, 1976–June 18, 2012
Loving husband of Holly, father of Philadelphia
Gone but not—

The rest is a blur through my tears.

• • •

There's no hurry. If you can't cry in a cemetery, where can you cry? The tears finally stop their steady stream maybe 20 minutes later. There's a soft white cloth in my satchel, the one I use to wipe my lenses, and it serves as a Kleenex. It's only as I give myself one last blow that I notice it, partially obscured by taller grass around the headstone: a tulip, Easter yellow, still in full bloom. An impossible sight in October. Isn't it? The flower stands out among the grass, bright petals against the gray stone.

It looks so beautiful, this vibrant symbol of life against so many symbols of death. Uplifting. A lightness in a dark place. I snap a shot that frames the tulip against the backdrop created by my dad's headstone. And all at once, I have my Vantage Point theme. I grab the Nikon from my bag and snap one more.

22 HOURS UNTIL VANTAGE POINT

"Yes," Glenys says, when I pitch her on my idea for the theme. "I think it's wonderful, Pippa."

And I'm off to capture in a few hours what my dad never got the chance to do in his lifetime. Documenting the hospital, chronicling its stories, the symbols of hope made all the more powerful because they're set against a backdrop of pain.

Lightness in a dark place. Light in dark.

Glenys has given me free rein to shoot wherever in the hospital I'd like. At first I just wander the halls, looking for inspiration. Then I get an idea— the pond. The hidden oasis for those who are sick. A retreat where they can forget about their illness, if even for only a few minutes. Framed against the tall reeds, the empty bench at first seems like a symbol of death. The way I first saw it. But now, I see it as possibility, as hope. As good will. A perch that offers respite to those who are sick, and those who are here visiting, loving them, for as long as they possibly can.

The crunch of gravel startles me.

"What are you doing?"

It's Ashley. You'd think the two cameras around my neck might be a dead giveaway. But I stifle a sarcastic response when I notice the green tint to her face.

"Are you OK?"

"No. Pretty much the opposite of OK. My friend had a party last night. Epic. But now I'm epically hungover. Can you take Mr. Winters to chemo?"

"I thought you loved doing chemo trips."

"Any day but today." She thrusts a clipboard at me then grabs her stomach with both hands and rushes down the hall.

Mr. Winters. Chemo. Again. Seriously? But I kinda owe Ashley for the panic-attack-in-storage-closet-with-Dylan day.

Mr. Winters is waiting in the chair at the end of his bed. I help him stand, making sure his tubes don't tangle, and we set off on the long walk from his room to the cancer center. I try to ask him questions as we're walking, to take my mind off things.

"Do you hate going for treatments?"

"No," he puffs. "It's not so bad. Only twice a week. And so far my white blood cell count has been pretty good. Only missed one treatment. At this rate I'll be done in two more weeks." His courage reminds me of Dad's. I guess he has to believe. What other choice is there?

The cancer center is eventually inevitable, a mere 10 steps away. The place I've managed to avoid for the past two weeks. Until now. Breathe in one, two, three, four, five. Out, six, seven, eight, nine, ten. Close my eyes. Then open them. That's when I notice how different the room looks. Not dark and cold and depressing, the way it used to be when Dad would come here, the few small windows on one wall the only source of natural light. Now, the room is bright, almost cheerful. I look up. Sunlight streams through three skylights, making the room come alive.

"Hang on here for a second." I put the clipboard down on the table inside the door to free up my hands, then aim the camera up, focusing on the bands of light streaming into the room, the background a haze. The perfect transition between light and dark. I come out from behind the viewfinder to appraise the rest of the room. Soft music plays. Not Pachelbel's Canon. Some music I'd expect to hear in a spa. Still *totally* inappropriate—since they've probably ruined aromatherapy massages for everyone in here for life. But at least it's not Pachelbel.

Oversized leather chairs still line the walls, their occupants hooked up to IV tubes, some of them with hands and feet in ice—to prevent their fingernails from falling out, I know. Lots of blankets, toques and scarves to keep their bodies warm. And an arrow at the end of the hall: radiation. That's all familiar. But the mood feels different. Or maybe it's just me. A new perspective? Who knows.

The nurse points us toward an empty chair near

the back and Mr. Winters settles in. He mumbles something, and I have to lean close to hear him. "The knitting basket," he says. "Can you get something for me?"

"The knitting basket?" I say, then try to mask my surprise by coughing.

"Yes, I know how to knit. My wife taught me years ago—she wanted us to knit each other slippers as a Christmas gift. I don't think she ever wore the pair I made her—making a pair of anything the same size is harder than it seems." He looks off in the distance for a moment, then snaps back to the present. "Never thought this would be the reason I picked it up again. Anyway," he sighs. "It's a communal basket. You just pick up where someone left off."

"Like, when they *die*?"

He just looks at me, the way people who say insensitive things tend to get looked at.

"Between treatments," he says. "Everyone shares in making the items—scarves, mittens, hats. Everything we make goes to help homeless people. Lets them know that someone's looking out for them."

Come on. Seriously? People who might not even make it themselves, sitting here, shooting up with near-lethal chemicals trying to kill the cancer that's killing them, worried about people who don't have enough money for warm clothes?

"I was working on an orange scarf. Can you see if it's there?" On the way back from the these-people-are-way-better-people-than-me basket, I remember the clipboard I left at the intake desk. As I'm grabbing it, a chart on the wall catches my eye, a list of patients' names in erasable marker. Under *Sunday 12:30 p.m.* is the name *Dylan McCutter.* And an asterisk.

I scan the board, looking for a clue, something, anything to tell me what's going on. In the bottom right-hand corner, the words are written like a death sentence: *final treatment.*

Dace and Mom are in the front seat of the Honda, chattering about the latest issue of *Vogue*.

"Are you OK?" Mom calls back to me, where I'm trying to focus on holding onto my display board to make sure it doesn't get jostled on the ride— but it's impossible to keep my mind off Dylan. He still hasn't replied to any of my texts. Cancer? Why wouldn't he tell me? Of course it makes sense. Why he hangs out in the atrium with the other cancer patients. How he probably really *did* fall asleep that night he stood me up. The bruises on his arms from being poked and prodded with needles. Why he deferred Harvard. How I never clued in to any of the signs. But the thing that keeps running through my head are the words *final treatment*. What does that mean?

When we get to the hall in Niagara Falls where

the competition is being held, there's a lineup of cars outside the door and kids unloading their unwieldy displays from the back seats. "I'll park and see you two in there," Mom says as she takes her place in the queue so I can unload. "Don't worry," she adds. "You're going to do great." They both think I'm nervous about my photos. They have no idea about Dylan.

How I just want to get back to the hospital in time to see him. But first, I have to focus on the competition. I head inside. Jeffrey is already setting up his display. Six mittens: red, orange, yellow, green, blue and purple. The rainbow effect is impressive.

I pull my board out of the protective plastic bag and set it up on the easel beside him.

"I heard what happened," Jeffrey says. "You OK?"

"Ask me in an hour," I say.

"You'll kick ass, Pippa," Jeffrey says, eyeing my photos. "You always do."

Ben saunters in, fancy black portfolio case in one hand, a coffee in the other. He pulls his foam board out of the case and mounts it on the other side of me.

I stare in disbelief at *my* photos.

"What are you doing?" My face hot. "Mrs. Edmonson said we had to start from scratch. That we couldn't use any of the photos she saw. That *you* couldn't use *my* photos."

"She also said she didn't want the judges to find out. So there's no way she'll say anything. And I knew you'd be too chicken shit to take a chance." He glances at my photos. "You must've been busy, starting over. Besides, who do you think she's going to believe the photos really belong to? Me, who stood by the photos right to the end, or you, who gave them up so easily?"

I remember what Mrs. Edmonson said. If the judges find out about this, we might both be disqualified. And if I rat him out, what's to stop him from saying I smashed the window of his SUV? "Why would you do this?" I whisper.

"Easy," Ben says. "The five grand." But there's something about his answer that makes me think it's not actually about the money at all. But I definitely don't care enough about Ben Baxter to find out.

A voice booms over the loudspeakers. "Welcome to the 15th Annual Vantage Point Competition." Cheers sound throughout the room, but I feel a million miles away. I look at the stage, where a man in a brown tweed suit and skinny tie is standing at the podium on stage.

"I'm Saul Ramm, dean of the school of photography at Tisch University at NYU. I'll also be one of three judges today, along with Gabrielle Brady and Lars Lindegaard, both of whom are professors in the program, and will be instructors at our prestigious camp. I'm thrilled to see what looks like our largest turnout yet from the Western New York region—and I look forward to seeing all of the talent in the room. Now for a bit of housekeeping. We'll be starting the judging process in 10 minutes, so if you're a contestant and you haven't set up your display yet, please make sure you do so," he says, scratches the top of his head, then turns the mic off.

I fidget nervously as the judges start to make

their way around. They reach Ben, and I watch as he explains the meaning behind *his* photos. The Nikon camera his grandfather gave him for his 13th birthday. The yellowed photo of his father as a young boy. The door to the hospital room he was in for six months after a near-fatal car accident last year . . .

I close my eyes, blocking Ben out, and channel Dr. Judy. Breathe, breathe, breathe. There's nothing I can do. What Ben does is out of my control. All I can do is focus on my own entry.

"Pippa Greene?" The woman with dark brown hair pulled back in a low ponytail is holding a clip-board. "Are you ready?" The other two judges stand on either side of her.

I take a deep breath. "My theme is Light in Dark." As the judges examine the board my own eyes flick from image to image. The sunlight streaming through the skylights into the cancer center. Mr. Winters, knitting the orange scarf. The yellow tulip set against the granite of Dad's gravestone. Howie, skateboard raised above his head—a picture I never thought I'd use, but that reminded me that light was there at the hospital, all along. I just didn't see it. The bench in the reeds. And lastly, the photo I found on the roll of film when I went to get it developed: Dad. He's propped up in the hospital bed against a mound of pillows, a container of chocolate pudding and that first copy of *The Catcher in the Rye* on his tray table. Unaware that I'm taking his picture, he's completely himself. His eyes are crinkled at the edges, and he's laughing. The last time I saw him truly happy.

"My father discovered he had pancreatic cancer

earlier this year," I tell the judges when they ask me whether I'd like to provide any context to the photos. "He was a photographer too. He received special permission from the hospital to capture the hospital's stories, but he—" I have to clear my throat. "He died in June. I didn't deal with that all that well." I clear my throat again, and cough, then brush away my tears with the back of my hand.

"I basically tried to ignore the fact that he was gone forever. But then I got assigned to do my volunteer hours for school at the hospital where he died. And I decided to attempt to do what my dad started—to show that this place that most people think is just about pain and suffering, is really about hope and having courage in the face of what, in some cases, are the worst possible circumstances."

● ● ●

The hour of judging is the longest of my life. Dace and Mom are standing on either side of me, their arms linked with mine. They're trying to distract me with idle chatter but I can't focus on anything else. Jeffrey's parents and his little sister, Rosie, are standing with him at his display. Ben is alone, talking on his phone.

"Are you sure you can't come?" he's saying. There's a pause, then he speaks again. "Yeah, but you could still make it to see the awards presentation . . . no, I get it . . . OK. Bye, Dad."

Someone taps the microphone and I turn my

attention back to the front. Saul is up on stage at the podium.

"I'd like to thank all the competitors, sponsors and judges who have made this year's Vantage Point possible . . ." he starts, but I tune him out as he rattles off the prizes I know by heart: first place wins $5,000 and a spot at Tisch camp. I'll settle for second—I don't even care about the $1,500 as much as I do about getting a spot at Tisch camp.

"This is it!" Mom whispers excitedly in my ear.

"All right, I won't go on any longer. We're ready to announce the winners," Saul says.

"I have chills," Dace says, unlinking elbows and grabbing my hand. "It's like the Miss America Pageant." I squeeze Dace's hand.

They start with the freshman/sophomore division winners, and everyone claps but I'm not really paying attention. Then finally, it's our turn. Saul clears his throat and rattles off the honorable mentions: "From Simon Chamberlain High in Buffalo, 'Transportation' by Ling Mao. From Westlane in Niagara Falls, 'Animosity' by Russell Cromwell. And from Spalding High in Spalding"—I hold my breath—"'Found' by Jeffrey Manson."

Jeffrey's parents cheer and Jeffrey runs up to the stage.

Either I'm going to Tisch, or I didn't even place. Ben's arms are folded over his chest. Will he beat me with my own photographs? The three honorable mentions stand for a photo with the judges, and collect their plaques and checks for $500 each.

They step away from the stage and Gabrielle steps up to the lectern.

"And now, for the top two photographers, who will be enrolled in the two-week intensive photography camp at Tisch. In second place, from Spalding High, 'Light in Dark' by Pippa Greene." Dace squeals and Mom squeezes me tight. It takes a second to register: I'm going to Tisch.

"And in first place, also from Spalding, 'Memories' by Ben Baxter."

Ben walks past me. "You coming?" he says. I follow him, stunned, up to the stage. But once I'm up there, the fact that he cheated and lied doesn't matter. I'm going to Tisch. I shake hands in a blur, accept my plaque and check, then beam uncontrollably for the camera.

When I get back to Mom and Dace, they both clobber me. Mom studies my plaque. "I'm so proud of you."

"We're going to New York!" Dace squeals.

I can't stop grinning.

"Who's hungry?" Mom says as we leave the building. "Pizza? The real deal, not the frozen stuff."

My thoughts go to Dylan. I check my phone. It's 2:30. "Can we stop at the hospital first? There's something important I need to do." Mom just nods. For once, she doesn't ask any questions.

•　•　•

I take the stairs up to the third floor, too impatient to wait for the elevator. I push open the door to the cancer center, expecting to see him right away, but he's not there. His treatment probably long since finished. I want to ask at the desk, to see if they know if he's still at the hospital but there's a line of patients waiting to be treated. I pull my phone out of my bag.

Me: Dylan! I'm at the hospital, are you here?

No reply. Callie will know. But in the caf there's another girl on cash. I'm standing there, trying to work out a new plan when Callie comes out of the swinging door beside the hot counter. She's drinking a Coke through a straw.

"Callie! Do you know where Dylan is?"

She looks surprised.

"I saw the board in the cancer center," I say. "I know."

She sighs, then nods. "Probably in the recovery ward. Back on the third floor, very end of the hall."

I race to the stairs, up to the third floor, down the hall, not letting myself think about what it all means. Past the nurses' station to the end of the hall, then to the end of the next hall. I find the door to the recovery room, second to the end, and push it open, only then realizing I probably should've knocked. The room is lined with beds, one after another. I scan the room, not seeing Dylan. Then, I spot him, at the very end, on the left side, by the window. He's sitting in a chair, reading. I rush over, and he looks up, startled.

"Hey," I say.

"What are you—"

"Why didn't you tell me? Are you OK?"

He puts his book on the windowsill.

"What's wrong with you? How did this happen? How long have you had cancer?"

Dylan bites his lip, watching me. Then he stands up and pulls another chair over. I sit down. So does he. He pulls his chair close, our knees touching.

"Back in the summer, I found a bump on the back of my neck. It started to swell, so my mom made me go to the doctor," he says. "They did some tests and figured out it was Hodgkin's. So since then I've been getting treatments. Radiation every day at first, for weeks. Now I get radiation twice a week and blood work once a week to see how I'm doing."

"So . . . you have cancer?" Tears well in my eyes.

He takes my hand. "It's a form of cancer, yeah. It's in my lymph nodes, but they caught it really early. It's a pretty common cancer in teens. But things are looking good. I didn't have to have chemo, only radiation, so I didn't lose my hair or have any of the really bad side effects, which is good, I guess."

"But on the chart it said today was your final treatment."

He smiles. "Yeah. Oh wait—not in a 'lost cause' way," he says, laughing, putting a hand on my knee. "Total opposite. They did more bloodwork just a few minutes ago, and I'll find out soon if I have to do any more treatments at all, or if they've gotten rid of all the cancer. I'm pretty optimistic. In young people they say it's highly curable, and that I could be totally cancer free."

"So . . . you're not a volunteer at all?"

He shakes his head.

"But not a deadbeat college dropout either?"

He laughs. "I deferred. To focus on getting better and to stay close to home. My mom was pretty shaken up. I'm sorry I didn't tell you, but I wasn't telling anyone, really. I didn't want their tilted heads, their sad, Poor Dylan eyes, you know?" He acts it out, and I let out a small laugh. "And you just assumed I was on the 'music team'—which by the way, is *so* not a real thing. And I remembered about your dad. And I didn't want to tell you I had cancer because, well, I didn't want you to think of me as nothing but a cancer patient."

"I definitely never thought that. With the bruises and the falling asleep and bringing Callie to the party. I thought you were a . . . slacker."

"I really did fall asleep. It's terrible. The radiation makes me so tired." He shakes his head. "And Callie's just a friend. Our moms are best friends. And even though she can be a bit *possessive*, she's really sweet. She's one of the only people who knows about the Hodgkin's, so it's just easy to be around her. I think I'm making her crazy talking about the elusive Philadelphia Greene, though." He looks at me.

Neither of us says anything for a minute. There's so much I want to ask him, but I don't even know where to start. So instead I reach over, tentatively, and grab his hand, then give it a squeeze. "I get it."

"I'm glad you know. Though I'm sorry this is how you had to find out."

He squeezes my hand back and then it dawns on him. "The competition! How was it?"

I smile. "Second place."

"You're going to Tisch?"

I nod.

"Stand up. I want to shake the hand of the most talented photographer I know."

I laugh as he stands, pulling me up, then grabs my right hand with his, shaking it goofily.

"Do you want to see my favorite photo from the display?" I ask once he's dropped my hand. I reach into my bag, and pull out the envelope with the duplicates of the photos I used in my entry.

He studies the photo of the bench. "Where it all began," he says, grinning.

"Where what did?"

"The relationship of Dylan McCutter and Philadelphia Greene."

"We're in a relationship?" I bite my lower lip, grinning.

"Philadelphia Greene, I think you're one of a kind. And you're going to New York." He shakes his head. "So impressive."

I can't stop grinning. "I owe you for the inspiration."

"Oh really?" He raises his eyebrows. "Because I can think of a way you can repay me," he says, playfully kicking my toe with the toe of his shoe.

"How?"

"By letting me do something I've wanted to do for a long time." He sets the photos on top of his book.

My stomach flips.

"What's that?" I say, but I know exactly what he's going to do. Finally.

"This," he says, sliding his arms around my waist and pulling me close. I reach up to put my arms around his neck, closing my eyes as his lips brush mine, lightly at first, then with more intensity, and then, I can't really think about anything else at all, and I lose myself in the moment.

CHANTEL GUERTIN'S **RULES OF ACKNOWLEDGMENTS**

1. Try not to forget to thank anyone. If you do, apologize profusely and offer to give them a Costco-size bag of Twizzlers. Hope they really like Twizzlers.

2. Thank your publisher, ECW Press: Jack David & David Caron for being the big men on campus; Erin Creasey for that very first email last summer, which was like getting a note in class from the girl you totally want to be friends with; Carolyn McNeillie for the perfectly Pippa cover design; Troy Cunningham for taking a bunch of loose pages and making them easier to read on a windy day; Jenna Illies for being captain of the pep squad (at a school where being on the pep squad means you're seriously

awesome); Jennifer Knoch for making sure sentences make sense; and Lesley-Anne Longo for catching typos. Also to the rest of the ECW crew for their support.

3. Give your editor her own number. Crissy Calhoun, you're a dream editor. Pippa is way cooler because of you.

4. Hug your family, for their love & enthusiasm: Michel and Susan Guertin, Danielle Guertin, Janet & Terry Visser, Sarah Farmer & Rob Newton. And my family to be, the Shulgans: Myron, Nancy, Mark, Jody, Cameron, Alice, Isaac, Julie & baby Junkin. Last but definitely not least, Myron & Penelope. I'm sorry there aren't any pictures in the book. Also, Mr. Baz, obviously.

5. Give xo's to early readers, researchers, and advice-givers: Heather A. Clark, Samantha Corbin, Melissa Di Pasquale, Melanie Dulos, Suzanne Gardner, Hayley Gillis, Leanna Gosse, Claudia Grieco, Sarah Hartley, Janis Leblanc, Jamie Lincoln and especially Marissa Stapley, for pool days and good juju bracelets.

6. Save the best for last: Chris. For the wintry weekend of editing in the woods. For driving around Schenectady on no sleep. For believing in me, loving me and making me laugh. For chest bumps and stormy squeezes. Love you, Shulgs.